JUSTICE LEAGUE

A GOLDEN OPPORTUNITY

by

MICHAEL TEITELBAUM

Based on a story idea
by Rich Fogel

BANTAM BOOKS
NEW YORK • TORONTO • LONDON • SYDNEY • AUCKLAND

A GOLDEN OPPORTUNITY

A Bantam Book/September 2003

Copyright © 2003 DC Comics. All rights reserved.
JUSTICE LEAGUE and all related titles, characters, and indicia are
trademarks of and © DC Comics.

All rights reserved. No part of this book may be reproduced or transmitted in
any form or by any means, electronic or mechanical, including photocopying,
recording, or by any information storage and retrieval system, without permis-
sion in writing from the publisher. For information address Bantam Books.

If you purchased this book without a cover you should be aware that this
book is stolen property. It was reported as "unsold and destroyed" to
the publisher and neither the author nor the publisher has received any
payment for this "stripped book."

ISBN: 0-553-48779-5

Visit us on the Web! www.randomhouse.com/kids
Educators and librarians, for a variety of teaching tools, visit us at
www.randomhouse.com/teachers

Visit DC Comics at www.dckids.com

Published simultaneously in the United States and Canada

Bantam Books is an imprint of Random House Children's Books, a division of
Random House, Inc. BANTAM BOOKS and the rooster colophon are registered
trademarks of Random House, Inc. Bantam Books, New York.

PRINTED IN THE UNITED STATES OF AMERICA

OPM   10 9 8 7 6 5 4 3 2

For the world's finest fans—you,
the readers of the Justice League

Special thanks to Rich Fogel for the idea; Keith Damron, Bruce Timm, and Warner Bros. Animation for merging the Arthurian and DC mythologies so beautifully on the JL animated show; Marissa Walsh of Random House for her input; and Paul Kupperberg of DC Comics for his encouragement and help in shaping the tale. —MT

PROLOGUE

Simon Rose was glad he had decided to take the job as the night security guard at Ancient Treasures, one of Metropolis's finest antiquities galleries. Since the death of his wife, Lillian, eighteen months earlier, the retired Metropolis police officer had had no idea what to do with himself. He managed to fill his days with hobbies and friends, but the nights were unbearably lonely.

When a friend had recommended him for this job, he figured he'd give it a try. He was still on his own, but as a lifetime lover of antiques, the idea of being among these prized items brought him some comfort, and he once again felt as if he was a useful member of society. Simon took pride in his new task, protecting priceless artifacts and works of art from ancient civilizations. He was giving something back to the hobby he so adored.

Simon strolled up and down the long aisles of the gallery, which had been converted from an abandoned factory years earlier to create this combination antique store and museum. He trained his powerful flashlight beam on the furniture, paintings, and small items brimming with beauty and history.

As he approached a short wooden stand on which rested a hinged gray box, a jolt of pain shot through Simon's head.

"Ahhh!" he cried, clutching his temples and dropping to his knees, as searing energy scalded his mind. Was this it? The dreaded stroke that he and his friends often joked about to keep the terror at bay? Would he soon be joining his late wife, his lost love?

Just as suddenly as it had arrived, the pain stopped. Breathing heavily, Simon regained his feet, wiping the sweat from his forehead with the back of his sleeve. Unexpected footsteps from behind a large oak dresser startled him and quickly turned his attention away from the painful episode.

"Who's there?" he shouted, waving his light toward the broad piece of furniture.

A woman stepped from behind the dresser. As her

face moved into the bright beam of Simon's flashlight, he gasped in disbelief.

"L-L-Lillian?" he stammered at the sudden appearance of his dead wife. "But that's impossible! How can you be here? This is insane!"

"I need you to do one last thing for me, Simon, my darling," the woman said in a whispered voice. "You have never refused me anything. But do this one final task, and then we can be together again. Forever."

With each passing second, the impossibility of his deceased wife standing before him grew less and less important to Simon. His desire to question this apparent miracle faded, and he wished only to be with her and grant her every request.

"Anything, sweetheart," he said, tears of joy streaming down his leathery face. "Tell me what you want."

Lillian lifted the gray box from its stand and handed it to her husband. Simon was surprised by the extreme weight of the object, and he rested it against his chest. "You must place this into the mailbox on the corner of Green Street and Kuhn Avenue in downtown Metropolis," she explained. "Just that. Then, my love, we will be together."

Simon glanced down at the box cradled in his arms. When he looked back up, his wife had vanished.

"Lillian?" he called, but got no answer. Gripping the box firmly, he slipped from the store and hurried down the street.

As Simon rushed toward downtown Metropolis, a small part of his mind tried to make some sense of his wife's mysterious appearance and her odd request. But each time he began to question the night's bizarre events, his mind was overwhelmed with thoughts of being reunited with his life's love.

As he neared the designated corner, Simon grew curious about the contents of the box. He had, after all, spent twenty-five years as a cop, and fifteen of those as a detective. Soon his curiosity got the better of him.

Pausing before the entrance to a massive skyscraper, he lifted the hinged lid of the battered metal box. Instantly, a brilliant light poured from within, stinging his eyes and flooding his mind with a torrent of images.

He saw a light-haired boy sitting upon a throne, looking out over the charred ruins of a once-great city. He saw armies of slaves, shackled and broken, marching endlessly to war. Finally, he saw the beautiful but cold face of a white-skinned, dark-haired woman cackling mercilessly at the torture of millions.

"No!" he yelled, his cries echoing among the empty

concrete canyons of Metropolis at midnight. *This box contains evil, pure evil.* "I can't do this . . . not even for you, Lillian. Forgive me, sweetheart. I've got to get help. Must find help."

Then, slamming the lid closed, Simon Rose staggered through the entrance and into the dark lobby of the skyscraper before him.

CHAPTER

1

The bright metal globe atop the Daily Planet Building glowed red, reflecting the crimson light of the setting sun. As many in the great city of Metropolis made the transition from day to night, from work to play, activity within the offices of the *Planet* was reaching its daily fevered crescendo.

Reporters hurried to put the finishing touches on stories slated for the edition of the paper that would go to press late that night. Layout artists pieced together the words, photographs, and advertisements that made up the great metropolitan newspaper. In the pressroom, the people who supervised the printing of the *Planet* prepared for another long night of work putting the efforts of the rest of the staff onto paper for the city to read the following morning.

On the thirty-third floor, Lois Lane, veteran reporter for the paper, dashed down a corridor, her latest story clutched in one hand, her coat and bag dangling from the opposite arm.

Lois loved her life as a reporter. It was all she had ever wanted to be, for as long as she could remember. Despite her confident, sometimes cocky attitude, she still woke up some days amazed and thrilled that she was actually a working reporter at the city's top newspaper.

A pretty, young copy editor with short reddish brown hair rushed up beside Lois, matching her long steps stride for stride. "Is that your feature on the homeless shelter, Miss Lane?" the woman asked.

"The very one, Kate," Lois replied, attempting to slip her coat on without getting either her bag or her story caught in the sleeves. "Ready to read it?"

"You bet!" Kate said eagerly, taking the papers from her as she helped Lois put her coat on. "Any chance to read *your* stuff, Miss Lane. It's like taking Journalism 101."

"Thanks, Kate," Lois replied, smiling. "You're sweet."

"Rushing off to someplace exciting?" Kate asked, imagining an exotic assignment filled with intrigue or danger. Kate was new on the paper and wanted to be Lois Lane when she grew up.

"Oh, not very," Lois replied with an exaggerated

touch of modesty. "Just heading over to city hall for an exclusive interview with the mayor."

"Awesome!" Kate said, turning left at an intersecting hallway, heading back to her desk. "Can't wait to read it! Good Luck!"

"But first," Lois said, pausing in front of an office door labeled CLARK KENT, straightening the collar on her coat, then brushing her stylish black hair from her forehead, "I'm going to pay a certain someone a little visit."

From the moment he had shown up at the *Daily Planet*, looking for a job that would allow him instant access to information on crime in Metropolis—the better to do his job as Superman—Clark Kent felt himself in competition with Lois Lane.

Not that he sought the rivalry. Clark had always considered himself a rather shy, self-effacing farm boy from a small town in Kansas, who just happened, in reality, to be the last son of the planet Krypton. But competition was a powerful part of Lois's nature, and in fact, it was one of the many things Clark found attractive and irresistible about her. So he didn't mind when he often found himself caught up in the glorious whirlwind that was Lois Lane. Not in the least.

What he did mind, at this very moment, was the "dog" of an assignment he'd been stuck with. The light-features editor was on vacation, and Perry White had asked Clark—whose resume included exposés of organized crime, daily journals of alien invasions, and exclusive interviews with Superman—to cover the Metropolis dog show earlier that afternoon.

"What am I going to write that hasn't been written about this a million times before?" Clark moaned to himself, shuffling through a stack of glossy photos of dogs of all breeds and sorting his hand-scribbled notes from the event. "Shelby, the smooth collie, wins Best in Show. Who would have thought it? Not me, that's for sure. I've never even heard of a smooth collie."

Tack-tack-tack.

A knock on the glass section of his door brought momentary relief from the drudgery of Clark's task. *Thank goodness for interruptions,* he thought.

"Come in," he said.

The door swung open, and in walked Lois, her coat buttoned, her bag slung over her shoulder.

"Hi, Lois," Clark said, brightening, as usual, at the sight of her. "I'll bet you heard about my lousy assignment and you've come to cheer me up."

Lois smiled and was about to speak. Clark interrupted her before she could get a word out. "No," he continued. "You feel so bad for me that you want to see if I'd like to grab some dinner before spending half the night finishing this feature."

"That would be awfully considerate of me, Clark," Lois replied, maintaining her tight-lipped smile. "But completely wrong. I'm here to let you know that, unlike you, I won't be spending half the night at my desk. I am on my way to an exclusive interview with the mayor."

She really can't resist competing, Clark thought, shaking his head. *I love it.* "Lucky Lois, interviewing the mayor," he began. "While poor, poor Clark is stuck here all night with giant schnauzers and miniature poodles."

"There's no luck involved, Clark," Lois said. "The best reporters get the best stories. Have fun with your puppies."

"Yeah, thanks," Clark muttered, watching as Lois quickly strode from the office. "Hey, how about a rain check on dinner?" he shouted after her.

"Good night, Clark," Lois called back as she disappeared into the elevator.

"G'night, Lois," Clark mumbled, getting up and closing his door. Returning to his desk, he turned back to his dog show notes. "'Rain check? Sounds great, Clark. Anytime.' Yeah. Right!"

Clark sighed, then returned to shuffling through the stack of photos.

The hours passed slowly. Clark had a sandwich delivered and ate it at his desk as he plugged away at the feature. As the hour approached midnight, the editorial offices of the *Planet* emptied out. Quiet settled in, and the only sound even Clark's superhearing could pick up was the dull staccato clacking of his fingers typing at superspeed on his computer's keyboard.

Shortly after midnight, Clark decided to wrap things up. He was almost finished with the piece and could easily add the final touches in the morning. Shutting down his computer, he gathered his things to leave.

BAM! BAM! BAM!

A loud knock startled Clark, who stood and rushed to his door.

BAM! BAM! BAM!

The knocker pounded even more urgently.

"Who in the world?" Clark wondered, glancing at his watch, then peering through the frosted glass with his X-ray vision, spotting an old man on the other side leaning against the door.

Clark flung the door open, and the man stumbled into his office, a look of terror splashed across his wrinkled face. The man's eyes bulged unnaturally, darting wildly around the room.

"Not safe," he babbled. "Evil, pure evil, if it falls into *her* hands . . . into *their* hands. The world . . . not safe."

Then the man pitched forward and fell, unconscious, into Clark's arms.

"Easy, now," Clark said, placing the man's limp body onto a sofa. Then he noticed the gray box that the man clutched tightly in his gnarled, bony hands.

KA-BASH!

Without warning, the door to Clark's office exploded, shards of glass and wood spraying everywhere, as two enormous creatures rushed in. The beasts stood eight feet tall and were clad in thick body armor. Their gray skin looked like stone, cracked and craggy. Enormous heads rested atop their massive bodies.

They drooled thick streams of yellow saliva from their apelike jaws protruding from beneath glowing red eyes. Each monstrous creature gripped the thick wooden handle of an enormous battle-ax, the sharp blade of which glowed with the same bloodred aura as its eyes.

Great Scott! Clark thought in the split second between the creatures' explosive entrance into the room and the realization that they were rushing toward the old man on his couch. *They look like giant ogres from a fairy tale,* Clark thought.

He stepped in front of the lead Ogre, intending to shove him aside before he reached the unconscious figure. Slamming Clark with his battle-ax, the Ogre easily swatted him away. The reporter went tumbling over his desk, stunned by the extraordinary power of this beast.

Leaping to his feet, Clark Kent swiftly scanned the entire thirty-third floor with his X-ray vision. Finding no one else nearby, he tore off his tie, shirt, suit, and glasses, changing into Superman in the blink of an eye.

Streaking across the room, the Man of Steel grabbed one Ogre by the neck and tossed him out of the office. The beast tumbled through a large, open newsroom, smashing into the far wall, then leaping back to his feet.

Superman reached for the second Ogre, whose massive hands were closing around the box still clutched by the unconscious man. The creature turned with greater speed than Superman had thought possible, and slammed the Man of Steel with his glowing battle-ax.

FOOMP!

Again, Superman went tumbling out of control, his mind racing. *What are these things? Where did they come from? And what do they want with the old man and that box?*

Just as he righted himself in midair, Superman heard the footsteps of the Ogre he had tossed heading back toward the office. Without turning, the Man of Steel swung his right elbow back, catching the charging creature in the jaw, dropping it once again.

By the time Superman flew back into the office, the second Ogre was clutching the gray box in his stony fingers.

"Aaiiiee!" it roared triumphantly.

Pouring on as much speed as possible in the limited space between the newsroom and his office, Superman tackled the Ogre around the creature's considerable waist, knocking it from its feet and sending the box skittering across the tiled floor with a metallic clatter.

After driving the beast into the floor, the Man of Steel turned, anticipating the attack of the other Ogre, who did not disappoint. Swinging his battle-ax at Superman's midsection, the Ogre caught the red-and-blue-clad hero in the legs as Superman tried to leap out of the way.

Superman spun out of control, smashing through what was left of the door frame of the office. As he got to his feet and shook off the latest blow, the Man of Steel saw both Ogres greedily grabbing for the box.

He swiftly pulled off his cape and sped through the air toward them. Reaching the grotesque duo, Superman whipped his cape around both Ogres, gathering its ends together with superspeed, scooping up the two beasts as if they were a giant sack of laundry. Maintaining a firm grip on the corners of his cape, Superman spun faster and faster into a blue-and-red blur.

"Aarrrr!" the Ogres cried, their roars of rage emanating from the makeshift bag.

At precisely the right moment, the Man of Steel released his grip on two of the cape's corners, sending the Ogres flying from the office. They tumbled through the air, then hit the floor of the newsroom, skidding across its slick tiles.

The momentum of Superman's powerful toss carried the Ogres all the way to the doors of the building's main elevator.

KA-RASH!

Their rocklike bodies smashed through the closed metal elevator doors. Down they fell, bouncing off the cinder block walls of the elevator shaft, plunging toward the roof of the car, which rested in the lobby, thirty-three stories below.

Reattaching his cape, the Man of Steel flew toward the elevator, through the gaping hole in its doors, then straight down the open shaft. When he reached the bottom, the Ogres were nowhere to be seen.

There's no way they could have gotten out of here!

he thought, looking around, unable to find any evidence that the beasts had smashed their way out through the thick walls. *But they're gone. Could they somehow have made it back to my office?*

Propelled by this thought, Superman flew swiftly back up the shaft and across the newsroom, landing in his office. There was no sign of the Ogres.

They've vanished! Superman thought, quickly scanning the building with his X-ray vision, but finding no sign of the man or the creatures. *How can they all have just disappeared?*

Then he remembered the box.

Superman found the battered box on the floor. Picking it up, he stared intensely at its dull metallic surface, attempting to see into it with his X-ray vision.

But no image clarified within his field of vision, just a dull gray blur. *Lead,* he concluded. *It must be made of lead. That's why I can't see through it.* Looking closely, Superman realized that the box was not locked. He had just assumed it would be difficult to open, and he wouldn't have wanted to risk tearing it apart for fear of damaging what was inside . . . or possibly unleashing some unknown danger.

"Sometimes the solution is right in front of your face," Superman muttered as he slowly opened the hinged lid.

Blinding golden light poured from the opening, washing over Superman. Images of death and destruction filled his mind, followed by an overwhelming feeling of tremendous weakness, as though his powers were draining from him like water leaking through a sieve. Just before the Man of Steel was about to black out, he slammed the lid shut.

Gasping, Superman leaned against his desk for support, feeling his sapped strength slowly return. "I think it's time to get a little help with this mystery."

CHAPTER 2

BEEP BEEP BEEP!

A piercing alarm split the Gotham City night. On a side street, the window of a small jewelry store lay smashed in a thousand bits on the sidewalk, glinting in the glow of a nearby streetlight. Around the corner, in a dark, narrow alley, five men dressed in black pants, sweaters, and stocking caps ran as fast as their legs would carry them. Each man clutched a small sack tightly, as if his life depended on it.

"I thought *you* were going to cut the alarm," the first man shouted as he ran, glancing compulsively back over his shoulder, then up toward the foggy rooftops. He knew that in this town justice did not always come in the form of police officers giving chase from behind. In Gotham City, he knew, justice sometimes came swiftly—from above. "With that racket, the cops will be here in no time!"

"No way, man," the second running figure said. "Jim was gonna cut the wire."

"Don't blame this on me," the third man said. "Who told you to hit that window so hard?"

"This is all messed up!" cried the fourth man. "Jim, this is all your fault."

"That really doesn't matter now, does it?" said a deep voice from above. The disembodied voice seemed to be moving along with the men, like a ghostly shadow matching their strides, no matter how fast they ran. "You'll have plenty of time to figure out whose fault it was where you're going!"

A shadowy caped figure appeared from the fog, materializing out of the misty air, swinging toward the fleeing men.

WHUMP!

The Dark Avenger dropped down on a thin line, slamming into two of the robbers feetfirst, knocking them into a brick wall on the side of the alley. They crumbled together in a heap.

"Batman!" gasped Jim. He ran faster, knowing full well he couldn't outrun the protector of Gotham.

Batman landed in front of him. Jim stopped short, then swung the bag he clutched at Batman's head. The

Dark Knight ducked easily, twisting into a backward, hands-first somersault, driving his feet into Jim's and a second man's chins. They dropped to the ground.

The final—and fastest—member of the quintet of thieves was almost out of the alley and around the corner. Batman pulled a Bat-bola from his Utility Belt, and after whirling it several times over his head to build up speed, he whipped it toward the fleeing thief.

WUP-UP-UP-UP-UP!

The weighted balls attached to each end of a rope sped through the air, finding the weapon's target and wrapping around and around the running man's legs, stopping their movement, and sending the thief sprawling to the cold, hard pavement.

Mopping the floor with two-bit thugs such as these took up a surprisingly large amount of Batman's time as the Dark Knight of Gotham. He much preferred detective work, analyzing clues, solving mysteries. But Batman knew that the Gotham City Police Department counted on him—albeit unofficially—to instill fear into the hearts of would-be criminals and to use the ones bold enough to attempt a burglary or mugging as examples to the others of his swift justice.

BOOWEE! BOOWEE! BOOWEE!

The sound of police sirens caught Batman's attention. With all five thieves immobilized, his work here was done. He fired a grappling Batarang toward the fog-laden rooftop, then scrambled up the brick wall of the alley, vanishing back into the night.

As Batman hoisted himself up and over the edge of the roof, landing on its smooth asphalt surface, the Justice League comm link in his cowl began beeping.

"Yes," Batman said crisply, never one for pleasantries.

"Batman," the familiar voice of Superman came through the comm link. "Got a bit of a mystery here I could use your help with."

For many years, the Man of Steel and the Dark Knight had teamed up, combining their skills and talents for such diverse purposes as capturing earthly criminals and fending off alien invasions.

Even before the formal establishment of the super-hero team known as the Justice League, the two costumed crusaders had come to depend on each other. Superman appreciated not only Batman's skill in combat, but also his keen mind and considerable prowess as a detective.

"Talk to me," Batman said, always intrigued by a mystery, although only an old friend such as Superman could detect any interest from his flat, even tone. The Dark Knight appreciated the amazing abilities of his friend from Krypton. He had learned from experience the many advantages that a hero with the powers of flight, superstrength, invulnerability, and all the other great gifts that Superman had could bring to a battle.

Superman recounted for Batman the strange episode with the old man, the lead box, and the giant Ogres.

Eyebrows raised beneath his cowl, Batman listened carefully to his friend's tale. He had been involved in many bizarre mysteries, but this unusual story intrigued him.

Batman knew that there were not many things in the universe that could harm or weaken the Man of Steel. When he learned that Superman had been overcome by the strange golden glow, the Dark Knight grew apprehensive, though he didn't share his concern with Superman.

"I'll meet you at the Watchtower," Batman said. "We can use the science labs there to investigate the box."

"Exactly what I was thinking," Superman said. "I'll contact J'onn and fill him in. See you there."

"Hmm," Batman mumbled, his nimble mind already running through the details of the case as he slipped from the rooftop, descending once again to the city below.

Orbiting above Earth, the gleaming space station known as the Watchtower functioned as the headquarters of the Justice League. Filled with state-of-the-art, high-tech scientific, military, and surveillance equipment, the Watchtower offered the heroes a safe meeting place and a research facility far more advanced than any available on Earth.

Funded by Bruce Wayne and built by his Wayne Enterprises corporation, the station's science labs contained the finest equipment and the combined knowledge of planets throughout the galaxy. The Justice League's private space shuttle—the *Javelin-7*—was available to all members for transport between the orbiting station and Earth.

Cutting its main engines and firing its retro-boosters, Batman eased the *Javelin-7* into the Watchtower's docking bay. The experienced pilot—who had flown everything from his supersonic Batplane to the one-man Whirly-Bat mini-helicopter—gently set the shuttle down, switched off the engines, then scrambled from the cockpit.

Meanwhile, Superman flew through space under his own power, with the mysterious gray box tucked safely away in his cape. The Man of Steel didn't need a vehicle to navigate his way past Earth's atmosphere. He did, however, wear a small tube-shaped breathing device, about the size of a harmonica, which Batman had devised for underwater use, but which had been modified to allow Superman to breathe in the vacuum of space.

As the docking bay doors hissed shut behind him, the Man of Steel quickly made his way through the Watchtower's maze of corridors and levels, arriving at a science lab just off the station's main observation deck.

Batman was there, waiting, along with fellow Justice League members J'onn J'onzz, also known as the Martian Manhunter, and the Flash, the fastest man alive.

"What took you so long, Supes?" Flash asked, never one to pass up an opportunity to give the group's leader—or anyone, for that matter—a playful hard time. "You may be faster than a speeding bullet, but apparently you're no match for Batman in the *Jav-7*."

"It wasn't a race, Flash," Superman replied with a forced smile. Though he did not show it to his teammates, he was still somewhat shaken by the powerful force he had unleashed within the box. The Man of Steel, so accustomed to shrugging off attacks with his invulnerability, had never gotten used to the idea that there were forces in the universe capable of causing him harm.

"Allow me to have a look at that, Superman," J'onn said.

The Man of Steel pulled out the box and placed it on a flat scanning device. Flipping a switch, J'onn activated a scan ray, which moved slowly over the box, analyzing its structure.

"You say your X-ray vision could not see inside," J'onn said.

"That's right," Superman replied. "My guess is that it's made of lead."

"That is a correct assumption," J'onn said, checking the structural analysis of the metal box.

Adjusting the scanner's settings, J'onn switched the device over to its magnetic imaging capability to view the contents of the box. On the scanner's view screen, the four heroes saw the image of a magnificent golden crown encrusted with jewels of every color.

"Nice hat," said Flash. "I mean, it's pretty and all, but why all the fuss? Since when are we in the jewelry business?"

"It is not simply a hat, as you put it, Flash," J'onn replied. "The sensors indicate that the crown is emitting powerful energy of an unknown nature."

"Why would an old man in Metropolis be running

around with a golden, jeweled, energy-radiating crown?" Superman wondered aloud.

"Perhaps we should open it," J'onn said.

"Considering what happened to Superman when *he* opened it, do you think that's wise?" Batman asked, unable to mask the concern in his voice.

"Maybe not," Superman said, bracing himself. "But I'm kind of curious to find out what this is."

"If we are all agreed, then . . . ," said J'onn. The Martian Manhunter opened the lid and removed the golden crown from within. Blazing energy radiating from the headpiece flooded the room with brilliant yellow light. Its many jewels shimmered in multi-colored beams extending outward, sweeping over the walls and ceiling of the laboratory.

Once again, the Man of Steel felt his powers drain, growing weaker by the second, as hideous and frightening images filled his head. Terrible scenes also raced through the minds of his Justice League comrades, blood-soaked visions of war and devastation.

As a telepath, J'onn J'onzz experienced the horrible images more intensely than the others. After only a few seconds, he hastily dropped the crown back into the box and slammed the lid shut.

Batman and Flash each grabbed an elbow of the slumping Superman.

"I'm all right," he said, his strength quickly returning.

"What's up with the 'end of the world' slide show in my head?" Flash asked, his irreverence covering his fear.

"Those visions of terrible destruction . . . ," J'onn began. "They were quite powerful . . . and yet vaguely familiar."

"Is it possible that the crown contains kryptonite?" Batman asked. "That would explain a lot."

"No," J'onn replied, reviewing the breakdown on his scanner. "There are some stones with which I am not familiar, but no trace at all of kryptonite."

"I think it's time we learned where this crown came from," Batman said.

"My thoughts exactly," Superman added. "We need to head back to Earth."

"I'm game," added Flash. "And I can cover a lot of ground quickly, if we need that."

Batman nodded.

J'onn downloaded all he had learned so far about the crown onto Batman's minicomputer, then handed the Dark Knight a photo of the mysterious golden object, printed from the image on the view screen.

"I will remain here and continue to run more tests on the crown," J'onn announced. "Good luck."

Superman, Batman, and the Flash headed for the docking bay and the *Javelin-7*.

CHAPTER 3

"**W**here do we begin to look for info about this thing?" Flash asked as the *Javelin-7* approached Earth's atmosphere. He sat in the copilot's seat beside Batman, who was piloting the shuttle. "It's not like there's a Crowns 'n Things store at the mall."

"I've consulted with the curator of antiquities at the Metropolis Museum of Art on a few cases in the past," Batman explained. "He may be able to point us in the right direction."

"Good idea," Superman said. He'd been pacing nervously during the short flight, anxious to start finding answers. "Anyone who might shed a bit of light on this mystery is worth talking to."

"Sounds like a plan," Flash said, always reluctant

to let anyone, even his most respected teammates, have the last word.

Then the three settled into silence for the remainder of the journey.

A short while later, Batman guided the *Javelin-7* to a secluded spot just outside Metropolis. Easing the shuttle gently to the ground, he brought the enormous ship to rest among a grove of trees, where it would remain hidden from prying eyes.

"I'll fly Batman to the museum," Superman said to Flash as the three heroes disembarked. "We'll meet you there."

"I'll be waiting for you," Flash said. With a smile and a quick wave, he vanished in a streaking red blur.

Superman put an arm around Batman, then rose into the sky, headed toward downtown Metropolis.

"The Flash is certainly sure of himself," Batman pointed out as the skyline of the great city came into view beneath them. "Almost cocky."

"He's young," Superman said. "He'll learn."

"I don't remember ever being *that* young," Batman replied.

"I don't think you ever were, Bruce," Superman said, smiling sadly at his friend. "Come to think of it, neither was I," he added softly.

Among the many bonds the two great heroes shared were their unusual childhoods, their feelings of being outsiders. As a young boy, Bruce Wayne had watched in horror as his parents were murdered by a street thug. That event caused the devastated child to devote his life to fighting crime, and led to his career as the Batman.

Superman's childhood was even more unusual. Born on the distant planet Krypton, he was placed as an infant into a rocket and sent to Earth by his birth parents shortly before his homeworld exploded. Raised on a farm by adoptive parents, the Man of Steel was truly an outsider, not even of this world, but immensely grateful for the loving couple who had raised him on Earth. Still, he was always curious about his real parents and the world of Krypton.

Neither hero had asked for the great responsibility that they had chosen to shoulder, but both had come to accept their roles as defenders of justice. It was this, more than anything else, that had enabled the two men to form their strong connection to each other.

A few minutes later, the tall marble columns of the Metropolis Museum of Art came into view. The massive white building, home to some of the world's great treasures, sprawled at the edge of Centennial Park, the city's largest park.

As Superman drifted to the ground, placing Batman down beside him, he spotted Flash standing at the museum's entrance. The speedster's arms were crossed over his chest, his foot tapping impatiently.

"Nice of you to show up," Flash joked, glancing at his wrist, pretending to look at a watch that wasn't there. "You guys took so long, I think I became an antique myself."

"Follow me," said the Dark Knight, ignoring, as usual, Flash's quips and leading the way inside.

"Boy, he's cheery," Flash said as Superman walked past him.

"You should see him in a *bad* mood," Superman replied.

Batman led the way through the museum's main hall, where ancient suits of armor, swords, and lances greeted visitors. The building contained more than two million works of art spanning more than five thousand years of world culture, including paintings by great European masters, ancient African stone and ivory sculptures, priceless pottery from Asia, and the largest collection of mummies anywhere outside of Egypt among its many treasures.

On the top floor, the group trekked past a series of flags of ancient civilizations, hung from a row of flag-poles lining the wall. Nearby, a display filled with sculpted bronze demons and dragons made for an imposing sight.

"Nasty!" Flash commented, looking back at the grotesque figures frozen forever in time.

Batman turned down a narrow corridor, away from the display areas, to a suite of offices. Pausing before a wooden door labeled ANTIQUITIES-CURATOR, he knocked gently.

A soft voice from inside instructed them to enter.

Opening the heavy door, the trio strode into a small office crowded with artifacts. Its walls were lined with floor-to-ceiling bookshelves, overflowing with large leather-bound volumes. Stacks of papers and photographs covered every surface, and the room had the familiar musty smell of an old bookstore or someone's long-neglected attic.

At the far end of the office, practically buried behind piles of books and papers, sat a small man with long gray hair and a full, unkempt white beard. His clothes looked as if they belonged among the antiques, and his wrinkled, delicate fingers grasped a magnifying glass, through which he peered at a small stone sculpture of a cat.

"Hello, Dr. Milton," Batman said.

The man looked up from his work. "Well, Batman," he said cheerily, placing the magnifying glass down on his desk before standing and extending his right hand. "Always a pleasure to see you." He shook Batman's hand with surprising vigor for a man of his diminutive stature and fragile appearance.

"Doctor, we have problem," Batman explained, stepping aside to reveal his companions to the doctor.

"Well, well," Dr. Milton said brightly, extending his hand again. "Superman! This is quite an honor."

"A pleasure to meet you, sir," the Man of Steel said, taking the doctor's hand.

"Ahem." The Flash cleared his throat loudly. "Does anyone have a cracker? 'Cause I feel like chopped liver right about now."

Superman laughed. "I'm sorry. Doctor, this is—"

"The Flash," Dr. Milton completed the sentence. "Central City's protector, and the fastest man alive, right?"

"Well, yeah," Flash replied, surprise unmistakable in his voice. "Nice to meet you, Doc. I can see you're a man of taste."

"I must admit that I follow the exploits of the Justice League rather closely," Dr. Milton explained.

"A pleasant hobby and a welcomed diversion from my explorations into the past. I never miss an article in the *Planet* about your work.

"But you didn't come here to listen to an old man ramble. Tell me, what can I do for you?"

Batman pulled out the photo of the golden crown and handed it to Dr. Milton. "Can you tell us anything about this?" the Dark Knight asked. The doctor studied the image carefully, scratching his thick beard and going over the photo with his magnifying glass.

"How did you come into possession of this item?" asked the doctor.

Superman quickly recounted the events of the crown's delivery, carefully avoiding the details of his life as Clark Kent.

"It appears to be Welsh in origin," Dr. Milton began. "But it's difficult to pinpoint the exact time period or the specific royal figure who might have worn it. Some of the gems on this crown are quite rare and valuable, and a few I can't even identify."

Dr. Milton put down the photo and his magnifying glass. "I have a colleague who owns an antiquities shop here in town called Ancient Treasures," he explained. "He specializes in items from the British

Isles. I can think of no one better qualified to help you track down the origin of this—"

GRRRRR!

A guttural growl like that of a wild beast shattered the austere quiet of the curator's office.

Flash sped from the room and raced back through the narrow corridors. When he reached the display area, he was stunned by the sight of one of the bronze demons he had seen on the way in. The ancient sculpted creature had somehow come alive and climbed down from its perch on the wall, and it now snarled at the Flash, exposing its razor-sharp teeth and needlelike claws. Its face was a grotesque mass of distorted features, its body lean and muscular.

"Houston," Flash said as Batman and Superman joined him. "We've got a problem."

ROOOOAARR!

"More than one," Batman said.

As the sculpted demon closed in on the three heroes, a bronze dragon swooped down from above, unleashing a stream of fire, scattering the heroes and scorching the marble floor.

"What is going on?" Dr. Milton cried, catching up to the others.

"Get back, Dr. Milton!" Superman shouted. "I don't

know how, but somehow these statues have come alive!"

The terrified curator raced back to his office, slamming and locking the door behind him.

CLING CLANK CLING CLANK

"What now?" Flash asked, glancing toward the stairway leading up from the lower floors. As the metallic clanging grew louder, the heroes saw an army composed of living mummies methodically making its way up the stairs toward them. Each mummy grasped an ancient weapon in one hand and a shield in the other. The approaching collection of bandaged, rotted corpses banged the two together as they marched.

"I know museums are supposed to bring the past alive," Flash said, "but *this* is ridiculous!"

CHAPTER
4

The marching mummies advanced slowly but steadily, brandishing their weapons.

"We've got to neutralize those two," Batman said, pointing at the living statues, "so we can deal with that army."

"I'll distract the dragon," Flash volunteered, dashing right at the bronze beast.

The demon leapt onto Superman, its needle-sharp claws digging into his chest.

The Man of Steel cried out in pain, stumbling backward. Grabbing the demon by its arms, he struggled with all his superstrength to pry it loose, but found he couldn't budge the snarling beast.

Batman reacted swiftly, pulling a Batarang from his Utility Belt and flinging it at the growling bronze creature.

THWAK!

The spinning, sharp-edged disk struck the demon on the neck, slicing its gruesome head cleanly from its shoulders, sending it toppling to the marble floor, where it lay motionless. Superman tossed the once again lifeless bronze body aside.

"You okay?" Batman asked.

"I'll live," Superman replied. But even as the pain in his chest eased, the concern in his mind grew. He wondered how the creature had been able to hurt him so easily, but knew that an answer to this question would have to wait. He turned his attention back to the battle. "How's Flash doing?"

The Scarlet Speedster raced toward the dragon, his eyes locked on the creature's mouth. At the first indication that the dragon was about to unleash a blast of flames, Flash swerved to the side, avoiding the streaming inferno.

The dragon paused mid-flight, startled by the apparent disappearance of the crimson target that had been there just a moment before.

"You have *got* to do something about that breath, babe," the Flash said from behind the dragon. He had been so concerned about the creature's flame-throwing mouth that he neglected to focus on its whiplike tail, which swung hard and fast into his chest.

The Flash sailed through the air and over a nearby railing, the marble floor seven stories below rushing toward him.

Museum visitors, who had gathered in the main hall to watch the bizarre battle above, gaped in horror at the plummeting, crimson-clad hero.

FOOSH!

From the corner of his eye, Flash spotted a blue-and-red blur. When his downward plunge stopped, he found himself cradled in Superman's arms.

"Thanks, big guy," he said as the Man of Steel flew back to the top level of the museum. "Note to self: The back end of a dragon can be just as dangerous as the front."

By the time they landed, the army of living mummies had almost reached Batman. The Dark Knight tossed a Batarang at the flying dragon, but the beast melted it in midair with a stream of its fire-breath. It next unleashed another flaming blast right at Batman, who dove and tumbled out of the way.

Spotting a long, sharp lance in the hands of an

approaching mummy, Flash had a brainstorm. "Wait till you see me coming back," he said to Superman, "then distract the dragon."

Speeding toward the oncoming army, Flash snatched a lance from a soldier in the front line of marchers. "I'll just borrow this for a sec, if you don't mind," he said. "Or even if you do."

When Superman spotted the Flash racing back toward the dragon, he fired a blast of heat vision at the beast, which struck it in the throat. Annoyed, but unharmed, the dragon turned his attention toward the Man of Steel, unleashing a stream of fire. Superman leapt away at the last second, and the flames shot spectacularly over the railing, above the heads of the crowd watching below.

Running at blinding speed, the Flash speared the dragon from behind, driving the lance deep into its bronze body. With a final pained roar, the creature dropped to the floor, writhing in agony, then fell motionless.

Which is when the army attacked.

The undead soldiers swung their ancient blades at Batman, who ducked to avoid one swipe, then jumped up onto one of the flagpoles protruding from the wall to escape another.

Superman joined the fray, pounding two soldiers at a time with punishing blows, clearing the front line of advancing combatants.

"Argh!" the Man of Steel cried as a soldier struck him in the back with its sword. Although the blade hadn't penetrated his skin, Superman felt weakened by the blow. A second soldier followed immediately with a powerful swipe of its mace. Its spike-covered iron ball drove Superman to the ground. "Feel so weak . . . can't get up," he gasped.

Batman swung along the line of flagpoles, flipping from one to the next, grasping each with a gloved hand, then completing a full three hundred and sixty-degree circle with his body. With each completed turn, his powerful legs slammed into the approaching mummies, scattering them across the smooth marble floor.

I can't keep this up forever! Batman thought, swinging to another flagpole. As his hands gripped the long metal pole, he decided it was time to go on the offensive. Spinning around the pole several times, he forced his full weight toward the ground at the bottom of his arc while at the same time yanking on the pole with all his considerable strength.

KA-RACK!

The flagpole snapped from its mounting on the wall, and Batman landed in a crouch, clutching the long metal staff. He charged toward the throng of on-rushing attackers, carrying the flagpole like an over-sized lance.

One animated bundle of earth-stained rags stepped forward, its own lance extended before it, charging to meet Batman head-on.

"I can't believe this!" Flash exclaimed. "I know they call you the Dark Knight, but I never thought I'd see you in a jousting contest!"

Balancing the heavy pole as he propelled himself forward, making sure of his footing on the slick marble floor, Batman raced at his charging opponent, his cape billowing behind him as he ran.

At the last possible second, as the tip of the flagpole was about to strike the soldier, Batman twisted his body, turning the pole to the side so that it reached across the line of advancing mummies.

KA-LAANG!

Batman smashed a dozen soldiers with a single blow, separating them from their weapons and shields, sending the ancient metal artifacts clanging across the floor. But his strategy also had an unexpected advantage.

As the long metal shaft scraped against the metal of the weapons and shields, sparks erupted and splattered in all directions. Nearby soldiers burst into flames as the tiny friction-induced electrical charges tore through them.

"Nice shot, Bats," Flash called out. "And those sparks—"

"I saw them," Batman said, turning toward Superman, who lifted himself to his feet as his strength returned. "You okay?"

"I'm all right," Superman replied. "What did I miss?"

The final wave of soldiers began to spread out, surrounding the three heroes on all sides.

"Flash!" Batman called out. "See if you can corral them into a tight group."

"Yippee-io-kiy-ay!" Flash cried, then sped toward the perimeter of the approaching attackers. Running around and around the cluster of soldiers, shoving those who were moving away from the group toward its center, the Flash forced the remaining mummies to bunch together. He became a blurry crimson fence, restricting their movements.

"Superman," Batman said, pointing to the ceiling. "We need a live electrical wire to touch to the center of that group."

In a blue-and-red blur, Superman flew up to an ornate chandelier. Being careful not to damage what he assumed to be a priceless antique, the Man of Steel plunged his fist into the ceiling beside it, chunks of plaster and dust filling the air.

Grabbing hold of an electrical cable, he yanked it down through the hole. He then flew right at the center of the trapped soldiers, shoving the live wire into the open bandages of a writhing mummy.

ZZZAATT!

Sparks shot through the mummies, spreading quickly among the tightly grouped soldiers, turning their bandages into flaming torches. The creatures exploded apart, sizzling as they struck the floor. Within seconds, the smoldering army was reduced to a pile of ashes.

"I hope none of those exhibits are permanently damaged," Batman said as the smoke cleared. "We'll check back with Dr. Milton later. But for now, we should be going."

"Magic!" Superman cried as the heroes of the Justice League stepped from the museum.

"Excuse me," Flash said. "I mean, I love a good card trick as well as the next guy, but this is hardly the—"

"This must be some potent form of magic," Superman continued, ignoring Flash's quip.

"That would explain a lot," Batman agreed.

"Yes," Superman said. "Like the sudden appearance

and disappearance of those Ogres, the effect their axes had on me, not to mention what just happened here."

"What the heck is going on?" Flash asked impatiently.

"Superman is vulnerable to the effects of magic," Batman explained. "The Ogres' axes must have been magically charged. That would also explain the statues and mummies coming to life in the museum."

"And why their swords weakened me," Superman said. "It also explains why my heat vision didn't seem to harm that dragon."

"And it might also explain why *those* guys suddenly decided to take a stroll in Centennial Park!" Flash exclaimed, pointing to a thick grove of trees.

From among the trees, three large stone gargoyles, who had leapt from a nearby building, charged at Superman, Batman, and the Flash. The grotesque creatures of living rock carried long stone swords, which glowed eerily.

Panic swept quickly through the park as those enjoying the beautiful day fled in terror at the sight of hideous, sword-wielding beasts tramping through the lush landscape.

A bicyclist slammed on her brakes and skidded to the ground.

Two in-line skaters, both of whom had turned their

heads to look at the gargoyles, crashed into each other, their protective helmets clacking.

"What are those things?" an astonished jogger asked his running partner, swerving out of the way of the massive creatures.

"I don't know," his partner replied. "But I'm *sure* they're not allowed on the jogging path!"

Swinging their glowing swords and stomping across the park, the gargoyles sliced through trees and park benches in their way.

ROOOAAR!

Finding himself face to face with a statue of a long-forgotten mayor of Metropolis, one gargoyle roared in anger, then sliced the frock-coated sculpture in half at the waist.

That's when the gargoyles spotted the three heroes, who braced for an attack.

"Separate," Batman said. "Let's try to split them up."

Superman took to the air, flying at one gargoyle's midsection. "Steady," he said to himself. "Got to avoid that sword."

Spotting Superman's approach, the gargoyle raised his weapon. When the Man of Steel was within reach, the creature swung his sword at the streaking blue-and-red target before him.

But at the last second, Superman veered sharply

downward, flying mere inches above the ground. He grabbed the gargoyle's stony ankles and increased his speed.

Startled, the enraged beast growled in frustration as he swiped his blade downward, aiming for Superman's arm, but unable to reach any part of his attacker's body. The creature howled with fury.

THWAP!

Superman rammed the gargoyle into the thick base of an ancient oak tree, separating him from his weapon and rendering the beast unconscious.

Meanwhile, Flash sped around and around another gargoyle, slowing down long enough to create a tempting target, then increasing his speed as the beast repeatedly swung his weapon, hitting nothing.

"You call that a swing?" Flash said, unable to resist taunting his enormous opponent, confident that he could easily outrun any attack. "I swung better than that when I played Little League!"

The third gargoyle rushed at Batman. Timing his jump perfectly, the Dark Knight leapt out of the way of the creature's flailing sword, then somersaulted over his head, spun around, and locked his elbow around the beast's neck. Holding on tightly as the enraged creature tried to toss him off, Batman maintained his grip, like a rodeo cowboy on a bucking bronco.

While the gargoyle was busy trying to shake Batman off his back, the Flash sped up to it and grabbed the sword from his hands. "Yo, Supes," the Scarlet Speedster called out. "He's all yours!"

With the dangerous weapon now out of the gargoyle's grip, Superman flew with his arms extended and fists clenched before him like an arrow into the beast's bulky midsection with a crushing blow.

Timing his move perfectly, Batman fired a grappling Batarang, which caught the branch of a nearby tree. The Dark Knight released his grip on the gargoyle's neck and swung clear as the Man of Steel struck with devastating impact.

Still holding the glowing sword, the Flash sped back to the gargoyle he had been taunting. "Come on, rock boy," the Flash shouted as he charged toward the third and final creature. "Just you and me, a little one-on-one!"

The creature raised his sword and swung just as the Flash lifted the heavy weapon he was holding.

ZZZAT-PLOW!

The two weapons met, stone striking stone, sending flashing red energy beams spreading in all directions. When the brilliant light faded, the gargoyles were gone, vanishing as quickly as they had appeared. Superman lay sprawled on the grass.

Batman raced to his friend's side just as the Man of Steel began to stir. "I . . . I'm all right," Superman said as he climbed to his feet. "The impact of the two swords must have caused the release of magical energy," he said. Even as he spoke, he felt his strength slowly return.

"This is all tied up with that crown," Batman said as activity in the park returned to normal.

"Let's see if we can find some answers with Dr. Milton's friend at that antiquities shop," Superman said.

CHAPTER
5

William Van Nostrand peered over the top of his half-glasses at the silver sword before him. Holding a jeweler's loupe up to the gem-encrusted hilt, he scanned the line of blue and green stones, muttering "Hmm" to himself every few seconds.

Van Nostrand had opened Ancient Treasures thirty years earlier. During that time it had grown into one of Metropolis's finest antiquities galleries, and he had come to be respected around the world as an authority on all things British—the older, the better.

His gallery was huge, located in an old factory that had been renovated to accommodate the aisles and aisles filled with one-of-a-kind treasures from the mists of history. Ancient armor, costumes, pottery, tools, and weapons lined the shelves and filled the display cases of the cavernous gallery, along with rows and rows of bookcases housing original handwritten manuscripts, some dating back centuries.

Van Nostrand was a happy man, his love of the past having been his passion since childhood. He was never happier than when surrounded by these reminders of eras long gone.

But the past few days had been upsetting for the tall man in his sixties, with a full head of gray hair. A rare and valuable piece had been stolen from his gallery in the dead of night, and his trusted night security guard had disappeared around the same time, making the former police officer the prime suspect in the theft. Police had searched for the missing man, but he, too, seemed to have vanished into the darkness. Still, William Van Nostrand went on with his life's work and greatest passion—collecting, researching, and cataloging rare antiquities.

"Now where did that book go?" he said to himself, rolling back his old metal office chair. Van Nostrand stepped over piles of papers and boxes full of objects from many eras, all gathered in this gallery where the past had come to live on.

Scanning the thick leather-bound volumes piled up on the floor, he reached out for a book entitled

Sixteenth Century Weaponry. Sliding the musty tome from its place in a tall stack of books, the proprietor settled back into the squeaky chair and carefully opened the volume's yellowed pages.

He was interrupted by the sound of the front door opening. Over the years, William Van Nostrand had seen some strange things enter his gallery—artifacts from other ages, manuscripts from all over the world—but nothing in his experience had prepared him for the sight that came walking through his door at that moment.

Three costumed men entered the dark, musty building.

"May I help you?" Van Nostrand said, rising from his seat, squinting through the dim light. Then he recognized his unusual visitors.

"My word!" he exclaimed. "Superman. After all my many years in Metropolis, the famous Man of Steel walks into my shop. With Batman and the Flash. Well, what can I do for you gentlemen?"

"We're looking for the owner of this gallery," Superman explained.

"That would be me," the owner acknowledged. "I am William Van Nostrand."

"Mr. Van Nostrand, I'm a friend of Dr. Milton's," Batman said.

"Are you, indeed?" Van Nostrand asked. "I never knew that the esteemed doctor kept such exciting company when he wasn't buried in his books."

"He's helped me out on cases in the past," Batman continued, "and he suggested we speak with you."

Batman pulled out the photo of the mysterious golden crown blazing in its leaden box and handed it to Van Nostrand.

The frail-looking man turned pale and looked up from the photo at Batman. "This piece was recently stolen from me!" Van Nostrand exclaimed. "Do you gentlemen have it in your possession?"

"It's being held in a safe place," Superman explained. "What can you tell us about it?"

"Actually, I was researching the crown just before it disappeared," Van Nostrand explained. "It was part of a collection of clothing, weapons, and armor that I imported from Wales. That particular item was reputed to be the Crown of Pendragon, but its true origins are still a mystery."

"What's a Pendragon?" the Flash asked, noticing the stunned reaction on his teammate's faces. "Somebody want to clue me in here?"

"Pendragon is the family name of King Arthur," said Batman.

"You mean *the* King Arthur? Knights of the Round

Table, Excalibur, and all that knight-in-shining-armor jazz?" Flash asked.

"The very one," Van Nostrand said. "Artifacts from the reign of the Pendragon family are most cherished and difficult to come by. I was still investigating the authenticity of that piece when it was unfortunately removed from the gallery."

"Do you have any clues about who might have taken it?" Superman asked, hoping to learn the identity of the man who had stumbled into Clark Kent's office and was now recuperating in a Metropolis hospital.

Before Van Nostrand could respond, Superman dropped to his knees, his face a twisted mask of pain.

"Superman!" Batman shouted.

Superman threw his head back and lifted his hands to his face. "Arrrrgh!" He cried out in pain. Suddenly, jagged shafts of white lightning shot from his fingertips, slamming into Batman, driving the Dark Knight to the floor.

Flash sped to Batman's side.

"I'm all right," the Dark Knight said as the Scarlet Speedster helped him to his feet.

"But what's with Supes?" Flash asked.

Batman, Flash, and William Van Nostrand looked on in astonishment as Superman stood up, then began spinning at superspeed, like a living top.

"What's happening?" Van Nostrand cried, backing away from the inconceivable sight before him.

Bright light surrounded the Man of Steel, spinning in the opposite direction, first yellow, then red. Tendril-like threads of light wrapped around Superman, weaving together, creating a blanket of energy, covering him completely.

Slowly, the spinning stopped, leaving Superman encased within a gray cocoon. Its surface was uneven, its texture rough, and no part of Superman's body was visible.

Batman approached the enormous shell cautiously. He ran his hand along its craggy exterior, feeling for a seam of some kind, but found none. "Superman!" he shouted, hoping that his voice would penetrate the thick layer, and that his friend within was still alive and conscious. "Superman!" he yelled again, pounding on the cocoon with his fist.

The cocoon remained motionless and silent.

Pulling a sharp-edged Batarang from his Utility Belt, Batman sliced horizontally along the cocoon's surface, hoping to cut it open. The metallic edge of his weapon screeched, then dulled against the tough surface.

"Do you have any cutting tools?" the Dark Knight asked William Van Nostrand.

The proprietor of the gallery nodded, then headed

toward the back of the building. He returned a few minutes later with a canvas satchel. Dropping the bag onto a work table with a dull clang, Van Nostrand pulled out a long, thin metal tool with an electrical cord attached at the bottom.

"It's a diamond-tipped drill," Van Nostrand explained. "It can cut through even the hardest material."

Plugging in the drill, Van Nostrand revved up its spinning diamond tip, then pressed the tool against the cocoon. Sparks flew as the tip spun, its motor struggling to provide enough power. After a couple of minutes, he shut down the drill and looked on with dismay at the surface of the shell, which remained unblemished, as if no attempt to cut it open had been made.

Van Nostrand next pulled out a welding torch.

"Hey, careful with that!" Flash exclaimed. "I know Superman's supposed to be invulnerable, but we don't know what might be happening to him inside that wrapping."

"This tool has great precision," Van Nostrand explained, slipping on his welder's mask to protect his eyes and firing up the thin blue flame. "Shield your eyes."

A thin beam of searing heat blasted the cocoon's surface, moving across the tall gray shell. When Van Nostrand shut down the torch, the surface again looked untouched.

"Let me take a shot at it," Flash demanded, stepping up to the cocoon and placing his hands on each side of the tomblike enclosure.

Using his incredible ability as the fastest man alive, the Flash focused all his speed into his hands, vibrating them at a blinding rate, creating friction, which he hoped would burn through the outer shell. His hands blurred into crimson patches, moving faster and faster.

Smoke rose from both sides of the cocoon, giving Flash momentary hope that his plan had worked. But when he removed his hands, Flash discovered that the only things burning were his gloves, which withered away in brown wisps of smoke.

The cocoon remained unchanged.

Flash turned to Van Nostrand. "You wouldn't happen to have an extra pair of bright red gloves somewhere in this joint, would you?" he asked, not really expecting an answer.

"I'm going to contact J'onn on the Watchtower," Batman said, switching on his comm link.

"Yeah," Flash said. "Maybe he's got a clue about what's going on, 'cause we sure don't."

"Batman to Watchtower," the Dark Knight spoke into his comm link. "Are you there, J'onn?"

"I am here, Batman," J'onn replied. "I've been

wondering about your progress. What have you learned about the crown?"

The Dark Knight quickly filled the Martian Manhunter in on the bizarre battles at the museum and in Centennial Park, their discovery of the antiquuities gallery, and William Van Nostrand's belief that the object in their possession was the Crown of Pendragon. He then told J'onn about Superman's situation and their attempts to free the Man of Steel from his cocoon.

"My guess is it's another magical attack," Batman concluded.

"Not necessarily," J'onn replied over the comm link. "Don't forget that although Superman looks like a human, he is in truth an alien life form."

"Sheesh!" Flash said, joining the conversation via his comm link. "You make him sound like some kind of hideous beast that bursts out of people's stomachs!"

"I, too, am an alien life form, Flash," J'onn J'onzz reminded his teammate.

"And a heck of a good-looking guy," Flash replied, embarrassed that he had, once again, spoken before thinking. It was a constant problem for the young hero, whose mind sped along as quickly as his feet.

"His extraordinary powers serve as a constant reminder of the fact that he is from a distant planet, and his makeup is not that of a human," the Martian Manhunter said. "As he is the only survivor of the planet Krypton, neither we, nor even Superman himself, really knows all that much about his own physiology. It is possible that Kryptonians undergo a midlife transformation."

"You mean like a caterpillar changing into a butterfly?" Flash asked, his mask unable to hide the puzzled look on his face.

"For one example, yes," J'onn replied. "But Earth is not the only world in which some species experience this type of change. Back on Mars, our scientific databanks contained records of many races from a number of worlds who formed some type of cocoon-like cover and emerged in a different physical form."

"I don't know if wings would be a good look for Supes," Flash said. "No offense to Hawkgirl."

"So what now?" Batman asked.

"Since we really don't know what it is we are dealing with," J'onn began, "I feel that it's too dangerous to disturb the cocoon or try to move Superman to another location. I believe we'll just have to wait and see what develops."

"I was afraid," Batman said in a tight voice, "you were going to say that."

CHAPTER

6

Not knowing what to expect from the mysterious co-coon, the Justice League alerted the police to help evacuate the immediate area around the gallery. And, with the first transmission over the Metropolis Police Department's radio network, word spread quickly that something strange had happened to Metropolis's greatest hero. The Man of Steel was in trouble, and the city he had saved countless times over the years rallied to his side.

A huge crowd formed outside the Ancient Treasures gallery. It continued growing, and soon the police arrived to set up barricades to contain the throng, which threatened to disrupt nearby busi-nesses and traffic in the downtown area.

Naturally, the story was big news.

A WGBS-TV news van screeched to a stop in front of the Ancient Treasures gallery. Leaping from the van even before it had finished moving, a young reporter wearing an open leather jacket over a white T-shirt hurried toward the police barricade, followed closely by his cameraman.

Clutching a microphone in his left hand, the reporter flashed his press credentials at a Metropolis police officer with his right, then signaled for the cameraman to follow. The two made their way through the crowd. When they reached the front door of the gallery, a second officer waved them inside, where they were met by a startling sight.

"Wow!" the reporter exclaimed at the vision of a seven-foot-tall gray cocoon balanced motionless among the rows of ancient artifacts. "And Superman is supposed to be inside that thing?"

"That's what came into the station," the cameraman replied, switching on his handheld video camera and focusing on the bizarre object before them.

The reporter ran a hand through his mop of thick dark hair in a repetitive but useless ritual to fix himself up before going on the air. His hair flopped back down into its usual position on his forehead.

The young man had grown up in Metropolis, and like so many people his age, he idolized Superman.

Although he had covered the Man of Steel in action many times, he still never got used to the fact that the Metropolis Marvel, invulnerable to so many forces, sometimes faced great dangers from threats both known and, as in this case, unknown.

"Okay," he said to the cameraman as he heard the tinny voice of his news director trill in the earplug that was his link to the TV studio. "We go live in five, four, three, two . . ."

The little red light atop the camera flashed on, and the reporter spoke to an anxious population.

"This is Snapper Carr, WGBS-TV, reporting live from the Ancient Treasures gallery in downtown Metropolis," he said in a voice that got at least an octave deeper now that he was on the air. "This building is filled with strange artifacts from around the globe and centuries past. But none more bizarre than the object behind me. Little is known about the gray cocoon that mysteriously appeared in this gallery about two hours ago. What *is* known is that Superman, defender of Metropolis, is trapped inside.

"Details are sketchy, but apparently some manner of energy force shot from the Man of Steel's fingers, then wove this unbreakable tapestry of terror, encasing Superman within. The Justice League have tried every method at their disposal to break the cocoon, but have been met with failure. We'll try to speak with them in a moment. Right now, I'm with the gallery's proprietor, Mr. William Van Nostrand."

The cameraman zoomed out a bit to include William Van Nostrand in his view. Van Nostrand stood beside Snapper Carr.

"Mr. Van Nostrand," Carr began. "What can you tell us about what happened here?"

The stunned proprietor ran a wrinkled hand across his haggard face. "Well, I was speaking with Superman, Batman, and Flash," he began, "when all of a sudden Superman collapsed. Beams of light shot all around the gallery, then they came together to form this shell around Superman. We tried everything from a diamond drill to a blowtorch, but nothing seemed to even make a scratch."

"Could Superman be undergoing some kind of transformation inside the cocoon?" Carr asked.

"I really don't know," Van Nostrand said, uncomfortable before the camera and unwilling to speculate on the meaning of the strange events unfolding in his gallery. "No one does." Then he turned away.

"I'm going to try to speak with Batman or the Flash to see if they know anything more," Carr reported to his viewers, signaling to his cameraman to follow.

Batman knelt beside the massive cocoon, various tools from his Utility Belt splayed out on the floor. Uneasy with sitting around waiting for something, or possibly nothing, to happen, the Dark Knight passed the time in what he felt was at least an attempt at being constructive. Since conventional cutting tools had failed, he now turned to the collection of devices available to him at all times, from the various compartments of the carry-along tool shop and weapons armory known as his Utility Belt.

One by one he used the implements to try to scrape, cut, sand, or burn off a small piece of the gray shell, in hopes of using his portable minicomputer—which was linked by a high-speed wireless connection to the vast resources of the Batcomputer back in the Batcave—to analyze the material from which it was made. A brilliant scientist, as well as a great detective and warrior, Batman never ignored a potential scientific solution to a mystery like the one he now faced.

Having unsuccessfully used blades, drills, even caustic chemical compounds, Batman now fired up a small acetylene torch.

At that moment, a throng of TV reporters poured through the front door of the gallery. Batman did his best to ignore them, but the eager group quickly surrounded the hero, thrusting their microphones in his face, practically knocking the flaming torch from his hands.

"Batman!" one reporter shouted. "Cat Grant, the News at Six. What can you tell—"

"Batman!" a second journalist interrupted the first. "Is it true that aliens were spotted in this neighborhood shortly before Superman was captured by the killer cocoon?"

"Is it possible the aliens were working for Lex Luthor?" barked another.

"What exactly are you trying to—"

From the corner of his eye, Batman caught a red streak moving between him and the gaggle of reporters.

The Flash, knowing how much Batman hated talking to the media, moved up and down the line of reporters, forming a one-man wall between them and his Justice League partner.

"Batman's busy," Flash announced, unveiling his irresistible, media-friendly smile for the cameras. "And it's not a good idea to bother the man when he's doing the scientific thing." Then, whispering conspiratorially, he added, "He gets kind of cranky."

Snapper Carr and the others looked back, hoping to catch Batman making a breakthrough, but the Flash gently but firmly herded the group away.

"I'll make a statement," the Scarlet Speedster announced, looking right into the half dozen cameras that now focused on him. "The truth is we just don't know. It could be some Kryptonian rite of passage or evolutionary step. For all we know, the big guy could emerge from that thing with iridescent wings or a couple of extra heads. Only time will tell. Thank you."

The media horde broke up slowly, then Flash sped back over to Batman's side.

"Thanks," the Dark Knight muttered, switching off his torch after another futile attempt to crack a sample off the cocoon.

Then he glanced across the room at the reporters who were on the air, speaking to their concerned audiences.

"Superman, man or mutant?" one reporter began. "As his good friend the Flash said, and I'm quoting here, 'only time will tell.'"

Snapper Carr also stared right at his viewers. "Well, there you have it, the Mystery of the Metropolis Cocoon, Day One," he reported. "Lots of speculation, little fact. But one thing you can be sure of: We'll be right here to bring you any developments, as they happen. This is Snapper Carr, reporting live for WGBS-TV."

The three television sets in Lois Lane's office were on constantly, each tuned to an all-news cable network. Often, Lois was on top of a story even before the networks picked it up. But it was also part of her job to keep one eye focused on the constant info-babble emerging from the tubes while the other was trained on her own work.

The past few days had been exhausting for the *Daily Planet's* senior reporter. Lois was pressed to finish writing up her exclusive interview with the mayor of Metropolis, yet four urgent stories in the past two days had called her away from the office, launching her into the next phase of the juggling act that was her life.

Lois banged away on her computer's keyboard, intent on wrapping up the feature interview before heading home for some much needed rest. Almost simultaneously, the three news stations flashed a special bulletin. This was not that unusual, and not enough to turn her attention away from the task at hand. Over the years she had developed the ability to write while she listened to the TV, her finely honed news filter set to pick up key words that signaled to her that it was time to pay closer attention. One such word blared from all three sets within seconds of each other.

"Superman."

Instinctively saving her work, Lois turned from her

computer, grabbing the remote and raising the volume on the first TV. Details of the incident at Ancient Treasures poured from the speaker. Any mention of the Man of Steel was enough to get her attention, but this time he was in trouble, and her deep feelings for the Metropolis Marvel propelled her into action.

Grabbing her notebook computer, Lois bolted from her office, rushing from the Daily Planet Building and into a cab. As the taxi sped toward the gallery, a feeling of dread overcame Lois. She cared greatly for the Man of Steel—loved him, in fact, although his life as a super hero made romance difficult at best.

Pressing the speed dial on her cell phone, Lois called Jimmy Olsen, the *Planet's* young photographer, and told him to meet her at the gallery, *now!*

The cab screeched to a stop in front of Ancient Treasures, and Lois dashed from the backseat. Flashing her press credentials, she hurried into the gallery. Spotting Batman, she walked briskly toward him.

"Batman," Lois called out, booting up her computer. "Lois Lane, *Daily Planet.*" She realized that Batman knew who she was. In fact, years earlier, she had shared a romantic entanglement with the Dark Knight in his identity of Bruce Wayne. But Lois felt uncomfortable using her personal relationship with

Batman as an excuse to approach the intensely private and media-shy Dark Knight with any informality.

Batman, because of his history with Lois, and his awareness of Superman's deep feelings for her, was more than happy to allow the longtime professional journalist to set the tone of all their conversations.

"Lois," Batman said, nodding. He then proceeded to fill her in on the events leading up to the formation of the cocoon, as she typed furiously.

As they spoke, Jimmy Olsen arrived, rushing to Lois's side.

"What kept you, Jimmy?" she asked.

The redheaded youth was already snapping a lens into the body of his camera as he replied, "Just a little high-rise fire in Bakerline, Miss Lane." He raised the camera to his eye and got to work capturing the cocoon, the gallery, and the general pandemonium on film.

"So nothing's been able to break through the shell?" she asked, turning back to her interview with Batman.

The Dark Knight shook his head. "I can't even chip off a small sample to analyze."

Lois Lane's instincts told her that Batman was holding something back, but she knew better than to press the guarded hero. As she swiftly wrote up her notes, hoping to get the story into that day's edition of the *Planet,* her concern for Superman grew. What if this time something had come along that was more than the Man of Steel could handle?

Pushing those thoughts from her mind, she turned to her photographer. "Jimmy," she called out. "Go get that film processed while I write this up. I'll e-mail the story in, but I want to stay here in case anything happens."

The young photographer nodded, then dashed from the gallery.

Suddenly Lois found herself surrounded by the crowd of TV reporters, who, having grown bored waiting for something to happen, saw a chance to make their own stories. Microphones were shoved in her face, and questions began flying.

"Miss Lane, is it true you're Superman's girlfriend?"

"Did he send you a note of some kind before the cocoon got him?"

"Any plans for a romantic getaway with the Man of Steel once this harrowing ordeal is over?"

"People!" Lois shouted in a commanding voice that instantly silenced the crowd. She pointed at the giant cocoon. "Let's not forget why we're here, shall we?"

Then she turned back to her laptop to complete her story.

The slightly stunned crowd of TV reporters proceeded to make themselves comfortable. Although nothing was happening at the moment, nobody wanted to leave and miss the eventual outcome of this bizarre story—whatever that turned out to be.

Lois realized that she, too, was not going to leave until this situation had resolved itself. She justified her decision professionally—she didn't want to miss covering any developments—but also knew that her feelings for Superman could not allow her to leave him in a time of great potential danger.

And so the vigil wore on, hour after numbing hour. Reporters and TV crews from more and more distant cities streamed in, and the fairly roomy gallery was quickly packed to capacity.

"I usually don't get this many people in the gallery in a whole month," William Van Nostrand said to the Flash.

"Well, how often do you have three members of the Justice League on display?" Flash replied, smiling. "And one of them in a cocoon?"

Batman pulled Flash aside. "I've got to take care of a few things, but I'll be back soon," the Dark Knight

announced. "Contact me on the comm link if anything happens."

"What's the matter?" Flash asked. "Leave the oven
on in the Batcave?"

Without a word, Batman slipped from the gallery.

It was nearly dawn when Batman returned. The
cocoon remained unchanged, and the Dark Knight
quickly grew frustrated that the excruciating waiting
game had resumed.

Empty pizza boxes and crumpled coffee cups piled
up in the corners as the army of media continued their
campout, refusing to leave and risk missing a story.

Jimmy Olsen returned, having gotten his initial
shots in to the *Daily Planet*, and took up the vigil
alongside Lois. The veteran reporter continued to jot
notes into her computer and refine her take on the
events of the past twenty-four hours, setting up a
story that would be ready to go once anything news-
worthy happened.

Then, without warning, a thunderous cracking
sound exploded in the gallery. Lois turned to see a
split forming on the surface of the giant cocoon.
Almost stampeded by the rush of media people, Lois
worked her way through the crowd. She didn't have

to tell Jimmy what needed to be done. He instantly began clicking off picture after picture.

A jagged crack zigzagged along the front of the cocoon. As it widened, blinding white light poured from within.

"Superman!" came the shouts from the reporters.

"Is he alive?"

"Anybody see anything?"

"Can we have an exclusive statement?"

This was more than Lois could bear. Over the years working as a reporter, she had developed a tough-edged exterior to shield herself from some of the terrible things she had to cover. And, at times, she might even have been a bit overbearing or insensitive for the sake of a story. But this headline-hungry pack, each trying to outdo the other in the face of the danger and uncertainty now confronting Superman, went beyond the limits of reasonable behavior.

"Will you please all back away?" she shouted at her colleagues.

"Why?" cried a TV reporter, emboldened by the excitement. He lowered his shoulder and pushed forward. "So you can get an exclusive?"

FOOOSH!

"No," replied the Flash, who appeared suddenly, stopping the reporter's advance. "Because Superman might need a little space, whatever shape he's in, when he comes out of that thing."

"But—"

"The lady said *back*," Batman snapped, joining his Justice League partner in holding the crowd at bay.

Lois turned to the cocoon, her heart pounding in her chest. *Will he be all right?* she wondered. *Will he still be Superman?*

A pair of hands from within gripped the sides of the crevice, tearing the cocoon in half. Then a figure emerged, coming forward surrounded by streams of crackling energy, as if lightning were outlining his massive physique.

"Look!" shouted a reporter. "Is . . . *that* supposed to be Superman?"

Lois Lane could only stare at the figure of Superman, who looked out blankly at the commotion before him. Something indeed was different. Every inch of his body, his skin, his hair, his costume and cape, had taken on a shimmering golden hue, as if he had fallen into a vat of gold paint.

Superman glanced down at his glowing hands. He looked up at the reporters, fear and confusion apparent in his eyes.

CHAPTER
7

A barrage of camera flashes and bright TV lights assaulted Superman, who raised his hands to his face and stepped back defensively. As the Flash kept the crowd back, Batman moved toward his longtime friend.

"Superman?" he asked, cautiously approaching the cowering golden figure.

ZZZATTT!

As the Dark Knight drew near, the fear in Superman's face turned to anger. He extended his arms and lashed out, firing searing lightning bolts from his fingertips. Batman dove out of the way, but was struck by an electrical charge from the unexpected attack. It sent him skidding across the floor and crashing into a nearby display cabinet.

The Flash sped up to Superman's side.

"Hey, easy there, Supes," he said. "It's us. Me, Flash, and your old buddy Batman. We're here to help you, okay?"

Again rage filled Superman's face, and he fired a lightning blast at the Flash, who sidestepped the charge, then dashed to Batman's side.

"I'm okay," the Dark Knight said, dragging himself to his feet. "But the same can't be said for Superman."

"He seems to not even know who we are," Flash said. "And he's got that lightning thing going on, which is a new twist for him. Not to mention the whole golden look."

Having apparently gained some confidence from the energy discharges emanating from his fingers, the golden-hued Superman stepped toward the throng of journalists, randomly firing lightning bolts. The crowd scattered in terror, thoughts of self-preservation replacing the urge to get a story.

Superman stomped through the gallery, an out-of-control beast indiscriminately destroying priceless artifacts and antiques.

William Van Nostrand ducked under his desk. When this madness had ended, there would be plenty of time for concern about the many pieces of history that were being destroyed. Right now, personal survival was his highest priority.

"Superman!" a high-pitched, firm voice called out from behind him.

The rampaging Man of Steel stopped his barrage and turned to face the dark-haired woman who slowly approached.

"It's Lois, Superman," the woman said softly. "You know me. We've been through life and death together, many times. And we've shared many years of . . . of friendship."

Superman stared blankly, tilting his head from side to side as if trying desperately to remember something, anything.

"Lois Lane," she repeated, thinking about her true feelings for Superman, which went far deeper than friendship. "You know, the *Daily Planet*?"

Fierceness overtook his expression once more, and Superman fired a pair of lightning bolts at Lois.

FWOOSH!

Traveling faster than the lightning, Flash gathered Lois into his arms and carried her across the gallery. The twin energy blasts passed behind him, tearing a hole in the front wall of the building.

"Thanks," Lois said, shaken, as the Flash set her

down. "It's just hard to believe that he doesn't recognize me."

"Something is very definitely wrong with the big guy," Flash said. "But what?"

"Over here!" Batman shouted, hoping to get Superman's attention.

It worked.

His face still twisted with rage, the golden Man of Steel charged toward Batman.

"As much as I hate to do this . . . ," the Dark Knight said when Superman was just a few feet away.

Batman flipped open a compartment on his Utility Belt and pulled out a gleaming green stone.

"Kryptonite!" Lois shouted from across the room. "But that could kill him!"

"Gotta trust Bats on this one, Miss Lane. I'm sure he's got a plan," Flash said. "I hope," he added under his breath.

Holding the golf ball-sized piece of emerald rock to Superman's face, Batman hoped that the kryptonite would have its usual effect on the Man of Steel, at least neutralizing him for the moment.

Superman gazed questioningly at the chunk of green stone, then swatted it from Batman's hand, sending it sliding across the room. Turning, he ran toward the gallery's main entrance, smashing through its glass-and-steel doors. Once on the street, he leapt into the air and flew from sight.

"Flash, let's go!" Batman cried, rushing through the gaping hole left by the Man of Steel. "The kryptonite had no effect! Now *we've* got to stop him!"

"Excuse me," the Flash said to Lois; then he tore from the gallery in a crimson streak.

Why can't I remember anything? the golden figure wondered as he sped through the streets of Metropolis, a shining projectile flying just above the snarled traffic and the crush of pedestrians. *They called me "Superman," but the name is not familiar. Nothing is familiar, not these so-called friends, or this city, or even . . . even who I am.*

Glancing down, he spotted the red-costumed speedster, who had referred to himself as the Flash, keeping pace as he dashed through the crowded streets, darting between cars and around people. Looking up, he saw the gray-clad man who had tried to attack him with the strange green rock. That one, who had called himself Batman, swung from rooftop to rooftop, attempting to keep pace.

They claim to want to help me. They say they mean me no harm, but how do I know if they are telling the truth?

"You keeping up with him?" Batman asked Flash through his comm link.

"That's not the problem," the Scarlet Speedster replied, dodging a man pushing a baby carriage on the sidewalk and two cabs in the street, all the time keeping Superman in sight overhead. "Where's he going? And what kind of damage will he do when he gets there?"

"Don't know," Batman said. He tossed a grappling Batarang to the edge of the rooftop in front of him, then swooped between the buildings, above the streaking golden figure. "I'm just trying not to lose sight of him."

"What was up with that kryptonite?" Flash asked Batman as he continued following Superman through the Metropolis streets. "Do you always carry a chunk in your Utility Belt in case Supes goes batty? Uh, no offense."

"No," Batman replied, dashing across a rooftop. "But with all the magic that's been affecting him lately, I wanted to be sure I could control him, if something went wrong when he came out of that cocoon."

"Too bad it didn't work," Flash said. "It didn't look like it had *any* effect on him."

"No, it didn't," Batman said, more to himself than to his comrade. He had already considered several possible reasons for the kryptonite's failure, none of which he was prepared to share at that moment.

ZAAT-THAM!

A blast of lightning from Superman's fingertips streaked toward the Flash, interrupting the comm link conversation. The Scarlet Speedster cut sharply to his right, outrunning the energy bolt, which tore a huge hole in the street.

"Leave me alone!" Superman shouted, his golden face a vision of rage.

Looking back over his shoulder, Flash saw the front wheels of a car vanish into the gaping crater, brakes squealing, a look of horror on the stunned driver's face. Extending his right leg, heel first, the Scarlet Speedster came to a sudden stop, then spun around, reversing his direction, racing back toward the plunging vehicle.

Reaching the car, he yanked open the door, pulled out the driver, and carried him to safety.

"Thanks," the shaken driver said as Flash set him down. "Who is that guy? He looks like—"

"I know," Flash said as the man's car vanished

down the enormous hole. "Long story, but right now I think you'd better see to your car."

ZIIT-THIP!

A follow-up lightning blast aimed at Batman sliced through his grappling line, mid-swing, then continued, slamming into the corner of a high-rise building, sending debris raining down onto the street below. Caught among the falling chunks of glass and steel, the Dark Knight plunged toward the sidewalk.

FWISH!

Spotting his partner hurtling toward the ground, the Flash raced the three blocks that separated them in a heartbeat, catching Batman just before he struck the pavement. Then he zigzagged his way through the avalanche of tumbling wreckage until both heroes were clear.

Doubling back, the Flash again sped through the falling debris, this time gathering up two stunned pedestrians—who stood, frozen with fear, gaping up at the plummeting fragments—and carried them to safety.

"This has got to stop!" Batman shouted into his comm link, once again taking to the Metropolis rooftops, as the Flash sped along below. "He's already five blocks ahead of us, and there's no telling what other damage he'll cause."

"I'm open to suggestions," Flash replied.

"Brace yourself!" Batman ordered.

"For what?" the Flash wondered aloud, his arms and legs furiously pumping.

Without replying, the Dark Knight dropped from above, landing on the Flash's back. From there, he climbed up, placing one foot on each of his teammate's shoulders, then stood, balancing himself as the Flash quickly caught up with the streaking Superman.

"You picked a great time to try out a new circus act," Flash said as Batman's boots dug into his shoulder muscles. "What exactly are you trying to do besides send me to the chiropractor?"

"Just keep up with him!" Batman shouted.

Looking up, the Dark Knight spotted the golden S symbol on Superman's chest, directly above them. Batman crouched, tensing his muscles like a coiled snake preparing to strike. With a powerful thrust, he sprang straight up, his massive leg muscles propelling him like a bullet toward the Man of Steel.

As he reached the flying golden figure, Batman grabbed Superman's waist, locking his arms firmly in place, then landed on his back.

Superman reached around, preparing to fire a lightning blast at Batman, who grabbed the Man of Steel's wrist and, with an ease that shocked the Dark Knight, prevented him from taking aim.

There's no way I should be able to outmuscle him, Batman thought as the golden Superman spun like a drill, trying to fling the passenger off his back. The Dark Knight held firm.

"Will you just talk to us for one minute?" Batman shouted, his arm beginning to weaken as Superman's hand moved closer. "Just listen to what we have to say. We are your friends. We mean you no harm!"

Superman's wrist broke free of Batman's grip, and the Dark Knight prepared for the lightning burst he was sure would follow. Instead, the Man of Steel slowed his flight and drifted downward, landing in a thickly wooded park. Batman jumped off his back just as the Flash zoomed up alongside them. The trio stepped into a dense grove of trees to avoid being seen.

"You remembered who you are?" Flash said enthusiastically, assuming that to be the reason Superman had landed.

"No," the golden man replied, his eyes darting nervously from one hero to the other. "I have no memory other than awakening within that shell. Fear and rage filled my very being, and I felt threatened by everyone near me."

"C'mon, Supes," Flash said. "We've battled aliens, super villains, creatures of all kinds. We've fought side by side. You don't remember *any* of that? And what's up with the gold? The whole Midas thing is a little weird."

Superman stared down at his hands, his smooth golden skin shimmering. An image appeared in his mind, hazy at first, as if materializing from the depths of his memory. "A crown," he said softly. "A golden crown."

Batman and the Flash exchanged quick glances.

"What *about* it?" Batman asked suspiciously.

"Shiny gold," Superman replied. "Covered with stones of many colors. I don't know what it means . . . but it's the one vivid memory I can recall."

"Then it probably *was* the energy from the crown that caused this," Flash said.

"You have such a crown in your possession?" Superman asked.

Batman nodded. "Maybe J'onn can help us," he said, his gloved hand rubbing his chin. He opened his comm link.

"J'onn?" Superman asked, clearly puzzled.

"Another friend of yours," Flash explained.

Batman contacted J'onn J'onzz aboard the Watchtower and brought him up to speed on their situation. "I suggest you perform a level four tele-pathic probe," the Dark Knight said.

"Understood," J'onn replied through the comm link.

"Probe?" Superman said, drawing back with concern.

"You won't feel a thing," Flash explained. "J'onn's a telepath. He'll just peek around in your noggin a bit and see if he can dust off the cobwebs."

Superman agreed, then closed his eyes. The image of J'onn's green face filled his mind, and the Martian's deep but gentle voice resonated within his head.

"Do not be afraid, Superman," J'onn's voice echoed telepathically in his mind. "Relax."

A calm washed over Superman as J'onn probed his mind. Vague images appeared to the Man of Steel; places, structures, even human faces floated in his mind's eye, but nothing definitive came into sharp focus—except the vision of the golden crown.

When the telepathic probe was complete, Superman opened his eyes and breathed deeply.

"He truly has no memory of who he is," J'onn reported via the comm link. "The inner depths of his long-term memory are blocked. The only clear image I received was that of the crown."

"I'm no telepath," Flash began, "but maybe if he saw the real thing, it might jog his memory."

"Yes," Superman said quickly. "That sounds right to me. Take me to the crown!"

Batman nodded, his eyes narrowing suspiciously. "I'll call the *Javelin-7*."

"The *Jav*—" Superman began.

"Never mind," Batman said. He pulled the remote-control signaling device used for summoning the Justice League's space shuttle from his Utility Belt.

Within minutes, the unmanned craft appeared in the sky above them, piloted from the ground by Batman. The shuttle drifted gently down.

"Nice ship," Superman said as the *Javelin-7* landed beside them.

"Thanks," said Flash. "I made it myself."

Batman pressed a switch on his remote, and the ship's hydraulic hatch lowered. Superman climbed aboard first, followed by the Flash. Batman stood at the bottom of the entry ramp, staring at the golden figure of his longtime friend.

"Care to join the party?" Flash asked, sensing that something was troubling Batman more than he let on.

Without reply, the Dark Knight slowly joined the others aboard the ship. The hatch slid closed with a breathy hiss, and the sleek shuttle blasted into space for the short hop to the Watchtower.

CHAPTER
8

Deep within a hidden fortress, not truly of this world, nor completely of another, a dark sorceress ran her thin fingers through her flowing coal black hair, then focused her icy gaze on the crystal ball before her. Her small green eyes narrowed, her vision piercing the smooth surface of the crystal, within which floated a series of images. Glimpses of ancient lands, stone castles, and armor-clad knights on horseback gave way to flashes of modern Metropolis streets, stores, and museums.

Finally, the image of the Justice League's *Javelin-7* streaking through space sharpened into focus within the mystic orb.

"At last, my son will take the Crown of Pendragon and claim what is rightfully his," the sorceress cackled, her ebony lips parting into a wicked smile.

The witch stood in the central room of her fortress before a tall wooden pedestal, which held the magic crystal. The large windowless chamber was constructed of enormous stone blocks, its ceiling rising twenty feet, curving on all sides into a dome.

Across the room, a red-and-blue-clad caped figure stood, surrounded by a transparent, yellow-tinted force field running from floor to ceiling. Imprisoned within the narrow tube of energy, the man saw and heard all that the sorceress did, growing angry at her cocky self-confidence.

"You are insane, Morgaine Le Fey," the prisoner said softly, and not for the first time since his capture. "Your plan to place your son on the throne of a new Camelot failed once, thanks to the Justice League. This time won't be any different."

"And who's going to stop me, Superman?" Morgaine asked the trapped Man of Steel, taunting him with a look of mock sympathy. "You? Your brave Justice League teammates? I think not.

"As we speak, your friends are bringing my son Mordred right to the treasure that will give him the power to rule over a new Camelot and, eventually, the world. With the power of this crown, our armies will be invincible!"

Superman thought of the images that had flooded

his mind each time he had gone near the golden crown—visions of war, death, and devastation.

"What makes you so sure that this crown has the power to do what you say it can?" he asked, his claustrophobic prison growing more oppressive by the minute.

"Long ago," Morgaine said, clearly relishing the power she now held over Earth's mightiest hero, "in the days of the first Camelot, the wizard Merlin forged the Crown of Pendragon, instilling it with powerful magic so that Arthur could rule as king without opposition. Over the centuries, as Camelot passed from memory, the crown was lost. I recently became aware of its energy and realized that it had the power to make my son invincible. My long wait is finally over. The Justice League will hand the crown over to me freely and willingly, and then victory will be mine!"

As he listened, Superman pressed his hands against the inside of the narrow, confining force field. A jolt of pain shot through his body as he made contact with the inner surface of the energy beam.

"Arrrgh!" he cried out in agony, far less used to the sensation of pain than most.

"What a pity that with all your great powers you are so vulnerable to magic," Morgaine cooed. "And my magic seems particularly potent against you. Perhaps because I've had centuries to perfect it."

"If you're so powerful, why didn't you just transport the crown directly here, as you did with me?" Superman asked. He wanted to keep Morgaine engaged in conversation, hoping she did not realize that he desperately sought a way out of his mystical prison. "You also seemed to have no trouble sending those Ogres to Earth."

"There are limits to my power, as great as it is," the sorceress admitted. "As the crown has magical energies of its own, I cannot simply use my abilities to transport it from Earth to this realm. I used a spell of illusion to get that old man to do my bidding, planting images into his mind that he could not resist. I then created a transportation portal inside a Metropolis mailbox into which I ordered the man to place the crown. I needed someone to physically place the object into the portal. Unfortunately, he fought my commands and brought the box to you instead."

"What about the statues and mummies that attacked us at the museum?" Superman asked, staring up at the ceiling, wondering if the tubular force field was open at the top. Using his superspeed, the

Man of Steel could fly straight up and through the fortress's stone roof.

If the force field was open at the top.

"I was able to bring those inanimate objects to life because they had no inherent magical power of their own," Morgaine explained.

"But why did you try to kill us at the museum?" Superman asked, using his telescopic vision to scan the section of roof contained within the energy tube. "By then the crown was safely hidden."

"Yes," Morgaine said coldly. "Which I learned by listening in on your conversation at the antiquities gallery. Up to that time, I thought that you still had the crown. When I learned that it was no longer in your possession, I realized that more drastic measures were in order."

"And so you created that cocoon and concocted a spell to have Mordred and me switch places," Superman said, finally grasping the full extent of this mystery. "You knew that if my friends believed that Mordred was actually me, they'd eventually bring him to the crown."

"How very clever," Morgaine said. "It's a shame that you must perish, along with the rest of the Justice League."

"I'm surprised they didn't see through your plan,"

Superman said. His telescopic vision revealed that the roof appeared to be free of the spell. He hoped his voice did not show the sudden excitement he felt.

"I blocked all of Mordred's memories save that of the crown," Morgaine boasted. "That way the telepath, J'onn J'onzz, could not discover the true identity of the one whose mind he was probing."

FWOOSH!

Sensing that Morgaine was distracted by her gloating, Superman leapt straight up into the air at super-speed. His fists clenched, he prepared to smash through the ancient stone at the top of the column of energy that formed his prison.

FZ-ZAAT!

"Ahhh!" the Man of Steel shouted, slamming into the force field, which sealed itself shut at the top seconds before he reached the roof.

"Your powers are useless against me!" Morgaine cackled as Superman crashed hard to the solid rock floor. "And when the crown is finally mine, I will teach you the true meaning of power!"

The sorceress turned back to her crystal and watched as the *Javelin-7* made its final approach to the Watchtower. "Your friends are playing right into my hands!" she announced, her thin piercing laugh echoing through the stone-walled fortress.

Descending slowly, the *Javelin-7* glided into the open docking bay of the Watchtower. With Batman piloting the ship, the journey from Earth had been quick and uneventful. The golden Superman sat in silence, no longer consumed by fear or anger, yet still troubled by his inability to remember anything about his life before he emerged from the cocoon.

The Flash sat beside him, sensing his unease, still aware that something about all this had struck Batman as not quite right. However, quiet reflection was not something that came easily to the Scarlet Speedster. His mind was a constant torrent of thought. He had great difficulty focusing on a single topic for any length of time, and most of the time whatever came to his mind came out of his mouth in short order.

"So, did this little bit of space travel jog any hidden memories?" Flash asked as the ship landed and Batman shut down the engines.

"No," the golden Superman replied. "Nothing fills my mind but the image of that crown."

"Well, you'll be seeing it soon enough, right, Bats?" Flash called out to the hero in the pilot's seat.

Batman merely grunted, clearly not wishing to enter this conversation. He completed his postflight checklist for the shuttle, putting the great ship into its standby mode, then sprang from his seat and opened the hatch.

The door hissed open, dropping down to form a short ramp connecting the passenger section of the ship to the docking bay floor. Batman strode quickly down the ramp, followed by Flash and the golden Superman.

"This is most impressive," the yellow-hued Man of Steel commented as the trio made their way through the connecting corridors of the mammoth space station.

"It's not much," quipped the Flash, "but we like to call it our high-tech orbiting headquarters."

Reaching a science lab just off the station's main observation deck, Batman, still grim-faced and tight-lipped, punched the entry code into the electronic security system. The lab's door slid open with a soft *swoosh.*

J'onn J'onzz ambled over from his research station to greet his arriving teammates.

"Superman," J'onn said. The Martian was startled by the Man of Steel's strange appearance, though his feelings remained safely hidden beneath his stoic Martian exterior. "It is good to see you, my friend. You have been through quite an ordeal."

"J'onn J'onzz," the golden hero said. "I feel as if we have met, although I have no true recollection of that."

"This is often the case with those whose minds I enter telepathically," J'onn explained. "Although, of course, we have actually known each other for years, Superman."

"We thought that if Supes saw the crown, it might help bring back his memory," Flash said. "Actually, it was my idea."

Batman rolled his eyes and crossed the room to join J'onn at his control panel. "Have you been able to learn any more about the crown?" he asked.

"No," J'onn replied. "I have not been able to match its energy signature to any in our database, nor have I been able to identify some of the stones."

"You've kept it in a safe place, I assume?"

"Yes," said J'onn, typing a coded sequence into the lab's main computer.

A loud humming filled the room as a square platform descended from the ceiling. Suspended in a stasis field in the center of the platform floated the lead box containing the mysterious object responsible for starting the entire ordeal. J'onn shut down the field, and the box drifted slowly to the floor.

"Are you sure about this?" J'onn asked Superman.

"The last time I opened the box, the crown's energy weakened you greatly."

"It's a chance I'm willing to take," the golden Man of Steel said, unable to take his eyes off the lead container.

J'onn nodded, then flipped up the box's hinged lid. He removed the gleaming crown and handed it to Superman.

Instantly, brilliant light flooded the room. This time, however, the blinding radiance appeared to be emanating not from the crown, but from the golden body of Superman.

Batman braced himself, watching as Superman's facial expression changed from that of slightly dull confusion to one of knowing evil.

"Mother!" the shimmering, distorted image of the Man of Steel shouted, exhilarated by the memories flooding back into his mind. "I have it!"

It was clear now to Batman that this man knew exactly who he was. It was also quite obvious that he was not the Last Son of Krypton.

"Flash!" Batman shouted. "Grab him! Now!"

Batman dove at the golden imposter's midsection as the Flash, reacting more to Batman's tone than to his words, dashed up to the strange shining figure, grabbing him around the chest.

The searing illumination in the lab grew brighter still, forcing Batman to shut his eyes. But he maintained his grip on the imposter. A strange sensation flooded over the Dark Knight, the feeling of moving rapidly through space, being pulled by a powerful force and taken on a journey beyond his control.

Opening his eyes, Batman found that his field of vision was still filled with blinding yellow light. Although he could barely make out his surroundings, it was clear that he was no longer aboard the Watchtower.

CHAPTER

9

Batman landed forcefully on a cold, hard floor. As his vision cleared, he could see that he was now in a large stone structure. Glancing up, he spied a high domed roof. The walls were covered with ancient weapons, giving the place the feel of an old-time dungeon. Leaping to his feet, the Dark Knight spotted the Flash sprawled on the stone floor beside him.

"Flash?" Batman said, kneeling down beside his friend.

"Did you get the number of that truck?" the Scarlet Speedster mumbled, grabbing both sides of his head with his hands. "I'm okay. But where—"

"I see we have unexpected guests, my son," said a thin, eerie voice from across the room.

Batman looked up, and Flash scrambled quickly to his feet.

"Morgaine Le Fey!" the Dark Knight exclaimed, seeing the sorceress standing before a billowing curtain of blackness, as if the room ended immediately behind her.

"Batman," the sorceress cooed. "I'm so touched that you remember me. I expected only to transport my son—and his prize—back to my fortress, but I suppose when you made your rude attempt to stop him, you and the other came along for the ride."

"I know I say this far too often," the Flash said, "but will someone please tell me what the heck is going on?"

Ignoring Flash's request, Morgaine Le Fey reached out and took the golden crown from the glowing figure before her. Instantly, the golden version of Superman morphed into his true form: that of a twelve-year-old boy.

"Welcome home, Mordred," Morgaine said warmly. "I believe you know my son, Batman, now that I have removed the illusion I had placed on him."

"Mother!" the boy cried, running over to the sorceress and hugging her tightly. "At last there is nothing to stop us."

"So, like, on a scale of one to ten of looniness,

these two are what? A twenty-seven?" the Flash whispered to Batman.

The Dark Knight said nothing, but stared at Mordred, recognizing the short, thin boy with long, light brown hair as Morgaine's son. He had encountered the sorceress and the boy during her previous attempt to attain a magical artifact that would give young Mordred great power—an attempt that was foiled by the Justice League.

"When placed on his head," she said, "this crown, which you so thoughtfully delivered into my hands, will give my son the power to rule a newly restored Camelot and, ultimately, rule all of humankind!"

"Where is Superman?" Batman demanded.

"You may see your friend before I destroy you all," Morgaine cackled, raising her thin, pale hand.

As she gestured, the veil of darkness behind her dissipated, revealing the remainder of the room, including Superman, who was still trapped within the magically created force field.

"Batman! Flash!" the Man of Steel called out, looking worn and tired from his imprisonment. "How did you—"

"Long story," Batman replied. "Are you all right?"

"I would be if there was a way out of this energy field," Superman explained.

"Nooo!" Morgaine's shriek startled everyone in the fortress, including her son.

"What is it, Mother?" he asked, frightened by her outburst.

Morgaine dashed the golden crown to the floor, sending its multicolored stones scattering across the room.

"It's a fake!" she blustered. "This is not the true Crown of Pendragon. It is an imitation made of cheap foil and worthless stones!"

Morgaine turned to Batman, her eyes enflamed, rage bristling in her voice. "This is your trickery, no doubt!" she shouted, raising her arms above her head.

"A team effort actually," Batman said, bracing himself for the coming attack. "I had a little help from a telepathic friend."

The sorceress formed a bloodred ball of radiant energy between her hands. Thrusting her arms forward, she flung the pulsating sphere at the Dark Knight.

Diving out of the way, Batman somersaulted back to his feet as the powerful energy sphere rammed into the wall behind him.

Morgaine's next magical blast shot from her hands, ricocheting around the room, eventually tearing a hole in the stone ceiling. Chunks of stone and clouds of dust rained down on Batman, who grabbed a nearby shield that was hanging on the wall for protection.

Clenching her fists, focusing her magical abilities on the objects in the fortress, Morgaine unleashed a barrage against the heroes. Flaming torches from all over the fortress leapt from their forged-iron wall sconces and flew at Batman and the Flash like fire-tipped spears.

Batman jumped straight up, allowing torches to pass beneath him. Grabbing hold of an ornate chandelier, he swung across the room, landing in a crouch, ready for the next assault.

Even Mordred was not prepared for the physical manifestation of his mother's rage. The boy ducked behind the hand-carved throne she had prepared for him in anticipation of gaining the crown.

The Flash, meanwhile, easily outran the streaking missiles, speeding around the room, sidestepping the projectiles. As he passed by the energy prison holding Superman, the Scarlet Speedster noticed that the force field appeared to flicker momentarily.

Superman, too, realized that the mystical barrier seemed to have weakened. Gathering his strength, the Man of Steel hurled himself, shoulder first, against the circular force field. As he struck the barrier, Superman felt his arm pass through.

Struggling mightily, he tried to push the rest of his body past the curtain of power, but it snapped shut, tossing him back. He collapsed to the ground, exhausted from the effort.

Morgaine released yet another round of magical force, this time chipping bits of stone from the very walls of the fortress, flinging them at Batman. He dropped to the ground, splaying himself out flat on his stomach, as the wave of jagged stones passed just inches above his back.

Flash appeared suddenly at Superman's energy cage.

"You almost made it through that time," the Scarlet Speedster said. "She's distracted trying to destroy Bats . . . not to mention completely insane. She's having trouble maintaining this force field at the same time she's flinging half the fortress at us."

"I've got to try again!" Superman said through gritted teeth. "It may be my only chance."

"Let me help," Flash said.

The Scarlet Speedster took off, running in a tight circle around the energy field.

It looked to Superman as if a thin red wall of color had been thrown up outside his prison.

Flash saw the force field flicker once again.

"Now!" he shouted, maintaining his speed.

Superman plunged his mighty fist through a weakened section of the energy curtain.

When he spotted Superman's blue-clad arm extending from the force field, Flash grabbed it, adding the power generated by his own speed to the Man of Steel's superstrength.

ZZZAT-FOOM!

Superman exploded through the magically constructed prison. He tumbled to the ground, with Flash landing on his back.

"Thanks," the Man of Steel said, feeling his strength return. "Let's go give Batman a hand."

The weakness in the force field that had allowed Superman to break free of his cage occurred because Morgaine had summoned a great surge of magical energy. Her power surrounded the main room of the fortress, peeling the many ancient weapons—swords, knives, maces, axes, lances, and spiked clubs—off the walls. The assembly of weapons sped toward one central point in the room: Batman.

The Dark Knight looked quickly over his left shoulder, then his right. Sharp, deadly objects flew at him from all directions. There was nowhere to duck, jump, hide, or swing out of the way.

In the split second it took for this realization to hit, Batman heard a welcome, familiar voice shouting, "Down!" Dropping to the floor, his knees pulled in to his chest, his head tucked down, Batman felt the weight of Superman's body landing on his; then he heard the clinking and clanging of the various weapons bouncing off the Man of Steel's invulnerable skin.

When the last sword had glanced harmlessly off Superman's back, the two heroes rose and were swiftly joined by the Flash.

"It's over, Morgaine!" Superman said forcefully, feeling much more confident challenging the sorceress as part of a team, despite his vulnerability to her magic.

"Wrong, Superman," Morgaine cried. Mordred ran from his hiding place to stand at his mother's side. "It has just begun!"

Crossing her arms over her chest, Morgaine threw back her head and let out a shrill, unearthly cry.

"Aaiiiee!" she screeched, her battle cry like the scream of a wounded animal.

The reflective glass surface of a large, ornately framed mirror hanging on the wall above the throne began to ripple, like water in a breeze. Answering cries coming from the mirror echoed the sorceress's shriek. Then a dark hole in the center of the undulating silver surface opened, and an army of Ogres, even larger than the ones Superman had battled earlier, came leaping through, one by one, their huge clubs raised menacingly, glowing with magical energy.

"Destroy them!" Morgaine ordered, pointing at the heroes, seeking vengeance now that her plan had been foiled. She once again erected a dark curtain of energy, stepping behind the veil along with Mordred, where they could observe the coming battle.

The first wave of Ogres rushed toward the trio as still more of the creatures poured into the room through the magical mirror, yellow drool splattering from mouths filled with rotten brown teeth.

"I guess working for Morgaine doesn't include a dental plan, huh?" Flash said, wincing at the sight of the hideous beasts.

"Watch out for their magically enhanced clubs," Batman cautioned.

"You don't have to warn me twice," Superman said, recalling his previous battle against Morgaine's Ogres.

"First things first," Flash said, spying a mace on the floor that had been propelled off the wall by the sorceress's tirade. "I'm going to stop any more of our gruesome friends from coming through that mirror."

Speeding around the edge of the army of Ogres, too fast for any of the beasts to stop him, Flash scooped the mace from the floor and continued on his way. When he had almost reached the enormous mirror on the back wall, he lifted the heavy weapon, then swung it forward, adding the force of his speed to the momentum of the mace.

KA-RASH!

The huge glass shattered, spraying shards in all directions, its massive frame tumbling from the wall. Camouflaged by the cloud of debris, the last Ogre through the mirror slammed Flash with his magically charged club, batting him across the room.

"Omph!" the Scarlet Speedster cried, the breath knocked from his body. Unable to breathe or find his footing, the crimson-clad hero watched helplessly as the far wall of the fortress sped rapidly toward him.

FWOOSH!

From the corner of his eye, the Flash picked up a streak of red and blue. Superman flew low, mere inches above the floor, and caught the Scarlet Speedster just before he hit the wall. He pivoted in midair, speeding out of the way of a blow from an Ogre's club.

"Thanks," Flash said weakly, regaining his breath, as the Man of Steel placed him onto his feet.

Meanwhile, across the room, Batman fired a wall-penetrating grapnel from a handheld launcher, straight over his head. The sharp-tipped dart, attached to a bat-line, pierced the stone ceiling, digging in and grabbing tightly. Leaping high and clutching the thin but strong line, Batman swung over the charging, infuriated Ogres, who swiped their clubs at the Dark Knight as he passed by, just out of reach.

As he sailed over the heads of the enraged creatures, Batman tossed several Bat-bolas down at them.

FWP-WP-WP-WP-WP

The speeding bolas wrapped around three or four Ogres at a time, tying them up, pinning their arms—and their magically enhanced clubs—to their sides.

With the Ogres' weapons neutralized, Superman took to the air again, flying above the army, unleashing powerful, devastating blows to the creatures. As each Ogre lost consciousness, his body shimmered out of existence, vanishing in a brilliant flash of white light.

"Well, that's convenient," commented Flash, now fully recovered and weaving between the beasts. "No messy bodies to step over."

"It also gives us a bit of breathing room as we reduce their numbers," Superman pointed out, uncorking a mighty blow to the head of an Ogre.

THUMPH!

As Superman completed the follow-through on his punch, an Ogre caught him in the back with a crushing blow from his club.

"Argh!" the Last Son of Krypton cried, tumbling out of control. He crashed into a stone wall, which came down on top of the fallen hero.

Batman, from his vantage point above the Ogres, shifted his weight in midair. The Dark Knight then swung on his grappling line, landing beside the pile of stone and dust under which the Man of Steel was buried.

One by one Batman tossed chunks of rock off the pile of rubble, trying to free his friend.

"I'll keep these guys occupied while you help Supes," Flash chimed in, running up to an Ogre who was headed for Batman, and stopping, making himself an easy target. "Hey, handsome, wanna go clubbing?"

The beast roared and swung his club at the Flash, who easily darted out of the way, the club smashing into the floor. Enraged, the Ogre followed the speedster as he led the creature away from Batman.

Appearing to be in ten places at once, the Flash repeated his trick of stopping right in front of an Ogre, then moving just enough to avoid the creature's weapon while remaining close enough to keep the beast focused on him, not Batman.

"Oh, man," Flash said as he stopped before an Ogre spitting drool as he roared. "Get a bib or something, will ya?" The beast swung his massive club like a baseball bat, but Flash sped ten feet to his right, then stopped suddenly and watched as the club smashed into the midsection of another Ogre, destroying the creature.

This distraction gave Batman enough time to dig through the rubble, clearing away hunks of stone until he reached the debris-covered Man of Steel.

"Are you all right?" Batman asked, helping Superman to his feet.

Brushing the pulverized rock from his eyes, the Man of Steel stood up, feeling his strength return. As kryptonite did, magic affected him quickly and powerfully, but wore off soon after the exposure stopped.

"I'm okay," he said sternly. "But it's time to end this battle."

"I can provide you with cover," Batman said. "They won't be able to use their weapons against you." Reaching into his Utility Belt, the Dark Knight pulled out a tiny round capsule, then dashed the marble-sized sphere against the hard stone floor.

F-IISSSSS!

Smoke poured from the tiny capsule, quickly engulfing the Ogres in a thick fog. Unable to see their adversaries, the Ogres grew confused, slamming into each other and lashing out wildly.

Using his X-ray vision to see through the billowing smoke, Superman flew swiftly around the room. Locating each panicked Ogre, the Man of Steel delivered crushing blows to the beasts, each one vanishing as it was struck, until the last beast had disappeared.

Seeing the tide of battle turn against her, Morgaine whispered softly to her son. "We have waited all these centuries to reclaim your throne, Mordred," she said in a soothing, maternal voice. "We will bide our time and return. I promise, my son."

Tears flowed freely down Mordred's face, the eternal twelve-year-old less at home with the concept of patience. "Noooo!" he screamed, his tantrum growing fierce, as Morgaine cast a spell and the two vanished in a bright flash.

"It's over," Batman said, realizing the significance of the sudden burst of light signifying the end—for now, at least—of Morgaine Le Fey.

"Yeah, except for all this," the Flash said, waving his hand to push the smoke away from his face. "Didn't you read the surgeon general's report on secondhand smoke?"

Speeding around the room over and over, he created a whirlwind, which sucked the remaining smoke up through the hole in the roof created earlier by Morgaine's magic blast.

"There's still one thing I'm curious about," the Flash said to Batman when he had finally come to a stop. "How did you signal to J'onn to substitute that fake crown for the real one? I was right beside you the whole time, and so was golden boy."

"When I asked J'onn to do a level four telepathic probe on 'golden boy,' as you called him, that was a prearranged standing code we have," Batman explained. "It let J'onn know that I wanted him to read *my* mind first so I could send him a message. When he did read my mind, I told him to prepare the fake crown and hide the real one."

"So, there is no such thing as a level four telepathic probe?" Flash asked, a bit embarrassed that he'd had no idea about Batman's coded message.

"Not that I know of," Batman replied, suppressing a smile at his cocky teammate's discomfort.

Superman turned to his longtime friend. "But how did you—"

The Man of Steel was interrupted by the sound of cracking stone. Looking up, he and the others saw that the fortress was crumbling.

"A final good-bye present from Morgaine?" Superman asked as a huge chunk of the roof crashed to the ground beside them.

"Let's not stick around to find out," Flash suggested as a wall on the far side of the room toppled toward them.

Superman led the way, flying swiftly toward an outer wall of the fortress and slamming a hole through the stone with his fists. Batman dove through the hole next, followed by the Flash, speeding away from falling rocks and rubble.

When Superman emerged from the fortress, he was surprised to discover that he was not outside in some remote forest, but instead back in the Ancient Treasures gallery in Metropolis.

The Man of Steel's sudden appearance startled William Van Nostrand, who was still busy cleaning up from the media circus that had overtaken his gallery. There was no evidence remaining of the cocoon that had caused such a commotion.

"Superman!" Van Nostrand exclaimed. "You look . . . well, you look like yourself!"

"Yes, Mr. Van Nostrand," the Man of Steel said,

smiling. "Gold was definitely not my color. I'm glad to be back, though I'm not quite sure how I got here."

Switching on his comm link, Superman attempted to contact his teammates. "Batman, Flash, are you all right?"

"We were just wondering the same about you," Batman replied. "Where are you?"

"At the Ancient Treasures gallery," Superman replied. "And you?"

"As soon as we left the fortress, Flash and I suddenly found ourselves back aboard the Watchtower," Batman explained. "In the lab where we were standing when Le Fey transported us."

"So we each ended up back where we were when she magically brought us to the fortress," Superman said.

"The more I think about it," Batman began, "the more I believe that the entire fortress was a magical construct that did not exist in our physical universe. When her spell ended, we simply returned to where we had been."

Van Nostrand stepped up next to Superman.

"Excuse me," he said softly. "I don't mean to interrupt, but do you have the Crown of Pendragon?"

"It's safe," Batman replied, having heard the

question over Superman's comm link. "But I think it would be best if it stayed on the Watchtower for safe-keeping. Bringing it back to the gallery would just put you in danger again. Superman can explain."

"Agreed," Superman said.

"I'm heading to the museum to check on Dr. Milton," Batman announced. "Meet me there when you can."

"Understood," Superman replied. "I'm just going to give Mr. Van Nostrand a hand."

With his superstrength and superspeed, the Man of Steel helped the proprietor right heavy statues, put books back in their proper places, and clean up the mess that had overtaken his gallery. As Superman worked, he filled the proprietor in on the strange events surrounding the crown.

Van Nostrand looked at the Man of Steel sadly. "The Crown of Pendragon is a prized piece," he said. "But its magical power makes it a danger. Please keep it safely hidden. I prefer to deal with antiquities whose magic lies in their history and beauty."

Superman arrived at the Metropolis Museum of Art and made his way up the wide marble stairs. As he walked past the exhibits, he was amazed to see that the many mummies that had come to life and attacked him were now quite still and well behaved, back in their rightful displays.

Reaching the top floor, he saw the bronze dragon and sculpted demon that he had battled, also quite harmlessly exhibited.

Arriving at Dr. Milton's office, Superman tapped on the glass door and was told to enter. Walking in, he found Batman talking with the doctor.

"Looks like everything's back to normal," the Man of Steel said.

"Yes, Superman," Dr. Milton agreed. "Amazingly enough. It seems that when the magic spell was released from the exhibits, they returned to their previous condition. It was easy to set the displays back up, as if the whole thing had never happened."

"Thinking back now, it almost feels like the whole episode was a dream," Superman commented.

"More like a nightmare," Batman said. "Thank you, Doctor. I'll see you again soon."

"Good-bye, Batman," the doctor replied. "Don't stay away too long. Your visits always add a little excitement to life among the dusty relics of the past."

The two heroes strode from the museum, into the lush green of Centennial Park

"I never got a chance to ask you how you knew that

the gold Superman wasn't really me," the Man of Steel said as the two heroes paused.

"Once we learned of the crown's origin, and knowing of your vulnerability to magic, I immediately thought of Morgaine Le Fey," Batman explained. "She's been trying to place her son on the throne of a new Camelot since the time of King Arthur. I just needed to go along with the investigation until she tipped her hand.

"As for the imposter, I thought from the start that the whole butterfly-like metamorphosis idea was a bit far-fetched, when J'onn suggested it, but I figured that there was no harm in letting Le Fey think that we didn't suspect her magical involvement. When the kryptonite had no effect on you, I was pretty sure that the golden version was an imposter, placed there to take the crown.

"But what clinched it for me was that the fake Superman didn't recognize Lois. I know how much she means to you, and I don't care what changes you go through. That's one woman you just don't forget!"

Superman smiled. "No argument there, my friend," he said softly. "No argument at all."

EPILOGUE

Clark Kent sat at his desk at the *Daily Planet,* busily typing away, putting the finishing touches on his dog show story. Somehow, after the events of the past few days, working on this lightweight story didn't seem so bad. He was pleased for a bit of boring normalcy in his world following the bizarre confrontation with the mystical powers of a dark sorceress.

His office had been cleaned up and repaired by the maintenance staff so that no signs were left of the massive struggle that had taken place there. Simon Rose, the night watchman who had brought the gray box to Clark's office, had been released from the hospital that morning, none the worse for wear and with no memory of his magically induced trauma.

Not even bothering to knock this time, Lois

Lane flung open the door to Clark's office and hurried in.

"Who's there?" Clark asked, looking up at Lois, but acting as if she were still on the other side of the door. "Lois? Well, of course you can come in. Be my guest!"

"Cute, Clark," Lois said. "I understand you had a bit of excitement here the other day."

"Really?" Clark replied innocently. "I wouldn't know. As soon as anything interesting or dangerous happens, you know I'm out of here, faster than a . . . well, as fast as I can leave. I heard a crash, and that was enough for me. I grabbed my laptop and went home to finish my story."

"The dog show story," Lois said pointedly.

"Right, the dog show story," Clark echoed. "Anyway, when I got home, I flipped on the TV and got hooked on the vigil at the antiques place. Something about Superman in a cocoon. I didn't really get what was going on, but it captured my interest enough so that my dog story got put aside. That's why I'm here finishing it up."

Lois tossed a copy of that morning's *Daily Planet* onto Clark's desk.

"If you're interested in 'getting' what was really going on," she said, "I suggest you read all about it in my exclusive in today's edition."

Clark glanced down at the top story. Above a photo of Superman breaking out of the cocoon, the headline read:

GOLDEN SUPERMAN OUT OF CONTROL!
A HERO GONE BERSERK!

EXCLUSIVE STORY BY LOIS LANE

Clark smiled. "Like you always say, Lois," he began. "The best reporters get the best stories!"

ABOUT THE AUTHOR

MICHAEL TEITELBAUM is the author of *Justice League: Secret Origins* and *Justice League: Red Justice* (Bantam Books). He has been a writer, editor, and packager of children's books, comic books, and magazines for more than twenty years. He has worked on staff as an editor at Gold Key Comics, Golden Books, Putnam/Grosset, and Macmillan. His packaging company, Town Brook Press, created and packaged *Spider-Man Magazine,* a monthly publication, for Marvel Entertainment. Michael Teitelbaum's more recent writing includes the Garfield: Pet Force books (a series of five titles); *Breaking Barriers: In Sports, In Life* (based on the life of Jackie Robinson); *Samurai Jack: The Legend Begins;* and *Batman Beyond: Return of the Joker* (all published by Scholastic); junior novels based on the feature films *Men in Black II* and *Spider-Man* (HarperCollins); and *Smallville: Arrival* (Little, Brown). Michael and his wife, Sheleigh, split their time between New York City and their 160-year-old farmhouse in upstate New York.

Frozen Buildings.
Chemical Spills.
Robot Umbrellas.

Just Another Night In Gotham City...

Join Batman For Two <u>NEW</u> CD-ROM Action Mysteries.

COMING IN SEPTEMBER 2003!

Uncover the clues. Crack the case. Foil the fiends.

Available wherever computer games are sold, at www.learningco.com, or by calling 1-800-822-0312

 © 2003 Riverdeep Interactive Learning Limited, and its licensors. © 2003 DC Comics. BATMAN is a registered trademark of DC Comics. BATMAN and all related elements are the property of DC Comics. ™ & © 2003. All rights reserved.

The Learning Company®